S0-AAD-916

missing
the
piano

Dear Mom and Alice,

Just thought I'd write to say hi. As you probably know by now, I'm at this school where everyone thinks they're G.I. Joe. My squad leader's a whale. He weighs about two hundred fifty pounds and looks like the Michelin Man. He makes me do a lot of push-ups. Next time you see me I'll probably be all muscular and I'll have to get new clothes.

You should see my hair. I look like Colonel Sanders' illegitimate son. My head is shaped like an acorn.

If you think of it, could you come out for a visit? Maybe the play will come to Milwaukee? ~~God I miss you guys. I cried yesterday.~~

Cosette, how's the show? Have you started a fan club yet? Don't forget to send me an autographed picture.

Love,
Mike

**also by
ADAM RAPP**

The Copper Elephant

The Buffalo Tree

missing the piano

Adam Rapp

HarperTrophy®
An Imprint of HarperCollins*Publishers*

*Special thanks to
Don Knefel, Lisa Pliscou, Anthony,
and my editor, Elizabeth Law*

Harper Trophy® is a registered trademark of
HarperCollins Publishers Inc.

Missing the Piano
Copyright © 1994 by Adam Rapp

All rights reserved. No part of this book may be used or reproduced
in any manner whatsoever without written permission except in the
case of brief quotations embodied in critical articles and reviews.
Printed in the United States of America. For information address
HarperCollins Children's Books, a division of HarperCollins
Publishers, 1350 Avenue of the Americas, New York, NY 10019.

Library of Congress Cataloging-in-Publication Data
Rapp, Adam.
    Missing the piano / Adam Rapp.—1st Harper Trophy ed.
        p. cm.
    Summary: When Mike's mother and sister go on tour with "Les
Miserables," Mike's father and his new wife enroll Mike in St.
Matthew's Military Academy where, facing brutality and ignorance, he
learns to survive.
    ISBN 0-06-447369-4 (pbk.)
    [1. Military education—Fiction. 2. Boarding schools—Fiction.
3. Schools—Fiction. 4. Family problems—Fiction. 5. Coming of
age—Fiction.] I. Title.
PZ7.R18133 Mi 2002   2001024596
[Fic]—dc21   CIP
                                                          AC

❖

First Harper Trophy edition, 2001
Visit us on the World Wide Web!
www.harperteen.com

For my mother,
Mary Lee Rapp

missing
the
piano

chapter one

To Lay Miss Rablays

I didn't realize how quickly the sun had started to set until Alice looped one up to the hoop from between her legs. The ball lingered around the rim for a couple of very long seconds, brushed off the red square, and managed to find its way through the net. The sky behind the backboard was about seven different colors. Alice's golden hair lifted from her head as she cheered the shot home.

We were playing H.O.R.S.E. Usually when I play Alice I shoot left-handed; partly because it gives my kid sister more of a chance to hang with me, and partly so I can work on my weaker-handed shots. Even though Alice is pretty small and shoots granny style, she's capable of getting on a roll and hitting three or four in a row. She has a knack for getting on a roll a lot.

Alice is five years younger than me. I always tell her that her name makes her sound like she's a third-shift waitress with microwaved hair and swollen ankles, but actually she's really pretty and smart for her age. Last year she did some summer stock in Sullivan, Illinois, where she played a young version of Wendy in *Peter Pan*. Not only did she know all of her zillion lines, but also everyone else's in the entire show. One performance, the stage manager got really steamed because she saw Alice lipping Captain Hook's monologue about walking the plank.

Mom chaperones Alice on all of her auditions. She usually does a number from *The Secret Garden* or *Annie*, like the "Tomorrow" song. She's done quite a bit of regional stuff at places like the Melodytop in Milwaukee and at the Marriott Lincolnshire.

Anyway, I was about to shoot one from behind the garbage can, when the phone rang. I lowered the ball and started to go into the house.

"Michael Jeffrey, the phone can wait," Alice said. "We have a barn burner here. H-O-R-S to H-O-R-S."

"Just keep your pants on, Sis. I'll be right back."

I ran into the kitchen to answer the phone. It

was Harisse, Alice's agent with the cartoon voice from the A Plus agency.

"Hi, Mike. Is your mother there?"

"No, she's not. She's at work. She went in for some extra hours today."

"Well, do you think you can pass on a message for me?"

"Yeah, sure."

"Now this is a real screamer. You should probably write it down."

"Okay. Hang on a second." As I was rooting through the top drawer of the china cabinet for a pen, I looked out the window at Alice, who was practicing a shot from the free-throw line. Behind her, the sun was setting even lower and the sky had turned to a deep orange with stripes of purple. Alice grabbed one of her rebounds, took the ball in her hands, and held it above her head and started talking to it like it was a little baby.

After a moment I grabbed a napkin off the table and picked up the phone.

"Okay. I'm ready for the scream," I said to Harisse. "Shoot."

"Well," she said, "your very talented baby sister just won the role of Little Cosette in the national tour of *Les Misérables*," she said slowly. "Make sure you tell your mother Little Cosette. Pronounce that really well, okay Mike? Tell her to call my voicemail to confirm that she got the message. This is really big. Little Miss Alice Tegroff's gonna be a star."

"Got it," I said, trying to write it all down, tearing the napkin where the ballpoint wouldn't give any ink. "I'll call her at work."

I called Mom's work and the switchboard operator patched me to her extension.

"Medical, Mrs. Tegroff."

"Mom," I said. "Guess who just called? You're not gonna believe it."

"Was it your father? The child support?"

"No, Mom. It wasn't Dad," I said. "It was Wilma Flintstone."

"Harisse?"

"The agent," I said.

Mom started chopping her breaths. I thought she was going to hyperventilate.

"What, Mikey. What? Tell me," she panted. "Did Alice get something?! Tell me!"

"Jesus, Mom, calm down. Calm down before you wake the Fleishmans." The Fleishmans are these people who live next door and sleep all the time. Their curtains are always drawn.

"Michael Jeffrey! You tell me this instant, or I'm gonna take the pancake turner to your butt when I get home."

"Oh, jeez, Mom. Don't scare me," I said. "You're too frightening to behold."

"C'mon Mikey," Mom pleaded, "tell me. Please."

"Are you gonna get me the new Air Jordans?"

"Whatever, Mike. Just tell me what's going on."

"Okay. Brace yourself. Prepare for anything, Mom. You know the business of *show business*, anything could happen. You say so yourself." I had to ham it up a bit more. Mom likes melodrama. "Alice just got the part of Little Cosette in Lay Miss Rablays," I said.

"In what?"

"Lay Miss Rablays."

"You mean *Les Misérables?!* Oh my God! Jeezus Christmas, Michael! You know what this means?"

"Harisse wants you to call her voicemail and—"

Before I could finish, Mom started spazzing out, hollering these frenzied jungle noises that yaks and baboons make on *Wild Kingdom*. I even heard the phone drop and scramble across the floor and all of the guards rushing to her rescue, probably expecting to find her bra ripped off, or an inmate torturing her with a toothbrush or something. Finally, she came back on the phone, panting.

"Okay, Mike. I'm gonna try and get off early. Marna might be able to come in for me. I promised the new receptionist that I'd go to that garage sale on Rooney Drive with her, but I'll try to be home early. Don't tell Alice! Don't tell your sister a thing! I want to surprise her. Get her some jelly doughnuts or something. But don't let the cat out of the bag just yet, okay, honey?"

"Got it, Mom."

Mom is the heart and soul of our entire operation. When she's not working, she's hauling me to basketball practice, or fixing one of her casseroles from the "Food" section of the *Tribune*, or cutting somebody's hair. She went to beauty school at some cosmetology college before nurses' training.

Once, she attempted to give me a permanent wave. She used foil hot rolls and these chemicals and this stuff called "sculpting yoke" which was supposed to be made from the pulp of avocados.

"Michael," she said, pasting the green stuff all over my scalp with a wooden tongue press, "you're gonna absolutely love this, honey. The girls are gonna be breaking down the door to get at you. I'm gonna have to buy another deadbolt just to protect you from getting trampled."

I was completely shocked when I saw myself in the mirror. I looked like a cross between Don King and a tired version of David Letterman.

Even though I wasn't supposed to tell Alice about getting Little Cosette, I did anyway. Unfortunately, I broke the news to her right as Mom was coming through the door with a box of Dunkin' Donuts and a fractured coffee maker plastered with electrical tape from the garage sale.

Alice was so excited that she didn't even notice Mom hitting me over the head with the box of doughnuts. She went into this strange kind of spontaneous audition, in which she relived a lost episode of *The Brady Bunch*: the one where Jan kisses Mr. Brady on the mouth and Greg has this conversation with Marsha about liking Don Drysdale's legs.

Mom and I were laughing our heads off, partly because of Alice's performance, and partly because Mom had managed to land a glob of jelly right on my nose.

A week later, Mom and Alice took off to Boston to join the tour. Before they left, Mom had one of her corny mother-son conversations with me about doing the right kinds of things while she was gone. She always gives these speeches about lifting the toilet seat and not swearing and helping out with the garbage and treating Rayne, Dad's new wife, with respect. She also had to throw in the bit about not telling Dad about her new boyfriend, Charlie, like there would be an outside chance that he'd even give a damn.

What's funny is that Charlie's last name is Brown, like in *Peanuts*. I get a big kick out of that. I mean, you don't run into people with famous last names too often. They're not really serious, Mom and Charlie, but I think she likes him. What I mean by *serious* is that I don't think they're riding the hobby horse or mixing fluids or anything like that yet. I think they just play canasta and watch television and listen to old Cole Porter records.

Charlie's a counselor at the prison, and when he's not working, he moonlights at a jazz bar on the east side. He can really play the saxophone. Mom says he always plays for all the nurses on his lunch break. I think that's why Mom started liking him, because he's musical. She's kind of a sucker for those jazzy types. That's why I can't really understand how she and Dad ever hooked up. The only time I've ever heard Dad sing was when he was humming the theme to *I Dream of Jeannie* in this weak falsetto that made him sound like one of those half-baked bearded guys from the Bee Gees. And sometimes he and Rayne will clear the living room and dance this terrible fandango to Spanish salsa music. They're quite a sight.

Sometimes, when Charlie Brown comes over, we go out back and play basketball. He's not very good, but he's big enough to make me work on my rebounding. Whenever I play him one on one, I tease him about his hair because he has one of those spongy Afros from the seventies. I tell him he looks like a character that got cut from the final animation reels of *Fat Albert*. He could have been the white guy who hung around with Mushmouth.

What's neat is Charlie knows I'm not trying to be a racist or anything. He knows I'm just kidding around. I tell him that his 'fro gives him four extra inches, and with all the extra height he should be able to slam dunk over me with no problem. He just laughs and tells me that he'd never be able to dunk because he has "white man's disease," and that he wears his hair like that because it makes him look like Gabe Kaplan, from *Welcome Back Kotter*.

He always tries to convince me that white guys can't jump, but I think that's a bunch of malarkey. I had the highest vertical leap on my eighth grade team and we had three black kids and two Puerto Ricans. In fact, if I was five or six inches taller I'd probably be able to slam dunk.

When Mom and Alice took off, I had to go stay with Dad in Chicago. Mom and Dad got divorced when I was five, and I really don't remember him living with us. Once in a while, when I pull out the old photo album, I look at this Polaroid of him giving me a piggyback ride. I'm in diapers and have on this humongous red cowboy hat that looks five sizes too big, and he has this smile on his face like he's laughing. I don't remember any of that, though, but sometimes it's just nice to look at the pictures.

You hear a lot of sad stories about divorced families: the dad who kidnaps his son and takes him to Australia in a laundry bag, or the mother who goes to court to get weekend visits and winds up having to live in a trailer park because of lawyer fees, or the kid who tries to blow his brains out with a pellet gun and winds up having to suck his food through a straw because his face gets wired shut for six months. I think all of that is a bunch of malarkey. I don't think my situation is dramatic at all.

I'm not too crazy about Dad's new wife, Rayne, though. In fact, I wouldn't mind if she was licked to death by a pack of wild dogs. She looks like hell's version of Vanna White. And she has this mustache that she bleaches with this Sally Hansen stuff, but it always grows back.

Her life should be a documentary for women who try to live like they're starring in their own real-life soap opera. She has a personal masseuse and a hired manicurist. She even has this really nice Colombian maid, Consuela, who does all of the housework and laundry while Rayne gets her cellulite treatments and shops for seven-dollar loaves of gourmet bread that taste like Elmer's glue. Consuela's the one who taught my dad and Rayne how to fandango.

One time, when I was visiting Dad, she freaked out because I borrowed her hairbrush and forgot to put it back on her vanity beside the miniature soap sculptures of geese. She started stomping all over the place, yelling at my dad as if I'd discovered her vibrator and put it in the refrigerator. After that, I was forbidden to wander around the house alone. I felt like I was trapped in a really nice concentration camp for up-and-coming, twelve-year-old future Congressmen who'd cheated on their taxes.

While I stayed at my dad's, I spent most of my time at the YMCA and worked on my jump shot. At the end of the season, Coach Forrestall told me that if I wanted to make it on the high school level I'd have to improve my shooting range. After fifteen feet, I was a complete wreck. So, that summer, I became a gym rat and expanded my shooting accuracy to close to twenty feet. I couldn't wait for Mom and Alice to come home from Boston.

I missed shooting around with Alice. I mean, she wasn't exactly what you'd call cut-throat competition, but I liked watching her shoot from her ankles, granny style, and she was pretty accurate, and she giggled and flounced around and really cracked me up. There's nothing like watching your kid sister flounce around and flash her cloudy eyes and shoot granny style; nothing like it.

One night, about a week before I was supposed to start at Catholic High, I got a call from Mom. Consuela handed me the phone.

"Hi, Mom."

"Hi, honey, how are you?"

"Fine," I said.

"Are you being nice to Rayne?" she asked.

"Yeah, Mom," I said, "we're really chummy."

"Are they feeding you okay?"

"Oh boy, it's like a regular smorgasbord around here. You should try Rayne's roast beef. It tastes like a catcher's mitt."

"Oh, c'mon, Mikey. It can't be *that* bad." Then she paused. I could hear static crackling. "Are you playing any ball?" she asked.

"At the Y. My jumper's improving. Close to twenty feet."

"That's great, Mike."

"How's Alice?"

"She's doing great. Just great. You should see her, Mike. You'd be so proud. She sings a beautiful solo called 'Castle on a Cloud.' You should hear her, Mike, she sings it so beautifully. She got a standing ovation last night. At the *Shubert Theater!* And the assistant stage manager gave her a white rose with a water tip. And I met a man named Grover. He's an agent. He's interested in working with your sister out here."

"Wow, sounds really nice, Mom," I said. "When are you coming home?" She didn't answer. I thought our connection had gone bad. "Mom, you there?" I still didn't hear anything, just some more static. "Mom?"

"Yeah, Mike. I'm here."

"When are you coming home?"

"Well, that's just it, honey. They like Alice so much they want her to stay on through Philadelphia."

"How long?"

"It's only six weeks."

"Only six weeks? Are *you* planning on coming home?"

"Honey, she's been offered the part for six more weeks."

"Well, can't *you* come home?"

"No, Mikey. I can't. Alee has to have somebody with her."

"Jesus, Mom, what am I supposed to do? Ride my skateboard to Joliet every morning?" I felt myself unraveling all over the place. "School starts next *week*."

"I know, honey," she said. "I know it does."

"Well, what the heck am I supposed to do, close my eyes, click my heels and *wish* myself to school?"

"I have to talk to your father," she said. "We'll work something out."

"I can't stay here, Mom. I can't. Rayne freaks out when I use her hairbrush. And I don't know anybody around here. The only person I know is this man with a gold tooth who hands out balls at the Y, and I haven't even caught his name yet." I made sure to whisper the part about hating Rayne.

"I know you don't care for Rayne," Mom said. "And I know you don't know that many people, Mikey. I know that. But you're great at meeting people, and there are a lot of really nice kids your age in the city. You can adjust. You've always been great at that. Think of all the summer camps you went to. You always wound up making some good friends."

"No way, Mom."

"Why not, Mikey? Why not? Just give it a try."

"Forget it!" I said. "This is a bunch of crap!"

"Michael Jeffrey, don't talk to me like that. I'm

your mother, for Chrissake." I didn't say anything. I just concentrated on the air in my lungs, how it felt trapped, like I was locked up in a closet.

"Do this for *us*, Mikey. For you, me, and Alice. Do it for *us*."

"Yeah, Mom. Whatever." I always say "whatever" when I'm steamed. We didn't say anything to each other for a minute. I started picking at my cuticles.

"I really miss you, honey," Mom said.

I didn't say anything.

"Alee says hi."

"Quit calling me *Alee*, Mom," Alice said in the background. "It's *Alice*." Her voice sounded like it was underwater, like she was a zillion miles away. It made me smile.

"Oh, you're not that old yet," Mom said back to her. "I still call your brother Mikey and he doesn't complain." It was kind of funny, listening to them argue over the phone and all. It made me want to be there with them.

"Alice says hi," Mom said back to me.

"Tell her I said hi," I said.

"I'll put her on," Mom said. There was a pause.

"Hi, Michael Jeffrey," Alice said.

"Hi, Little Corvette."

"Ha-ha, very funny. It's *Cosette*."

"Just kidding. How's it going?" I asked.

"I think I'm growing boobs," she said.

"Well don't let 'em get too big."

"I'm gonna buy a training bra. I wanna be perky."

Then Mom took the phone away.

"Okay, that's enough, Miss Puberty," she said to Alice. "Say good-bye to your brother and go get ready for dinner."

"Good buy to your brother," Alice shouted out, her voice seemingly fading behind a door.

"She misses you," Mom said.

"Tell her I miss her, too." I thought about little Alice under the lights, collecting roses and signing autographs, and blowing kisses and all of that Hollywood stuff. It made me kind of sad.

"I love you, honey," Mom said.

"Me too," I said.

"Can I talk to your father?"

"Yeah. Hang on. I'll get him. Tell Alice to send me an autographed picture. I'll put it in my trophy case."

"I will, honey. I will."

"Bye, Mom."

I gave the phone to my dad and asked him if I could go to my room. Rayne was standing in the hallway, adjusting the frame of this picture of her and Dad on top of a horse, wearing checkered cowboy outfits, hugging each other like a couple of lovebirds. When I walked by, Rayne asked me to keep my basketball out of the front closet.

When I got to the guest room, I plopped down on my bed and started to think. I could picture Mom ordering room service and drinking champagne from those miniature bottles they stick in your bathroom at those jazzy places like the Regency.

All of the thinking made me feel pretty sad. I couldn't help it, knowing that I'd be spending more time at Dad's house with his haunted love queen, Rayne. I pictured myself stealing all of her hairbrushes and soaking them in gasoline. Then I'd scorch the hell out of them and fling the melted plastic all over her paintings.

That night, Dad walked into my room. I was listening to my boom box. A song by De La Soul was playing. Dad reached over and turned the volume down and sat on the end of my bed. He ran his hands through his hair and began shifting his weight on the end of the bed.

"Your mother wants you to stay here," he said. The back of my throat filled with that alkaline taste that rises up just before you're about to puke.

"I know," I said. My head was really spinning. High school was supposed to be something you slipped into like a new cotton shirt, not a solo suicide mission into a straitjacket.

"Rayne and I have to do some talking." Dad had a knack of looking away when he was speaking to you, like he was ashamed of something.

"What about Joliet Catholic?" I asked.

"Son, Rayne and I both work in the Loop. We don't have time to haul you forty-five minutes south every morning. Down and back turns into an hour and a half, not to mention twice daily, and with rush hour you never know how long you can get tied up."

"It's only twenty-five minutes, Dad," I said. "You *know* it's only twenty-five minutes."

"Twenty-five minutes?" he said. "Who's doing your math, the Little Sisters of the Blind? Maybe the way your mother drives, but I remember it being closer to an hour."

"No, Dad, it's twenty-five minutes. I time it every trip."

I wanted to tell him *why* I timed it every trip: because I couldn't wait to get back to Joliet, and timing it somehow made me economize everything, it somehow made the trip shorter. I wanted to tell him that I hated it at his house. I wanted to tell him that I fantasized about lodging an ice pick in Rayne's jugular, that I entertained thoughts about melting hairbrushes and flinging the melted plastic all over her art collection. I wanted to tell him all of that, but I couldn't.

"Listen," he said, "there are a lot of good private schools here in the city. Rayne and I have to discuss some things. There are a lot of really good options around here for high school kids. Just relax. We'll take care of everything. Let's all take a night to think it over," he said. I nodded my head. My dad brushed my hair with the back of his hand. I like when he does crap like that, even though I'm older now, even though I think he's a bastard who screwed us over. He rubbed his hands through his hair again.

"Listen," he said, "you've got to get some sleep and I have some things to discuss with Rayne. I'll see you in the morning." Dad bent down and kissed my forehead.

"'Night, son," he said.

"'Night, Dad."

That night, I woke up around 3:00. I couldn't sleep. I couldn't stop thinking about missing Mom and Alice, and wanting to kill Rayne. All of these things revolved in my head like crazy. I felt like I was on that ride at the carnival with the floor that drops, where you spin around really fast and stick to the wall.

I had to go to the bathroom, so I quietly walked out into the hall. I heard some muffled voices talking behind Dad's bedroom door. I stopped breathing and tried to listen. I pressed my ear to their door. Rayne was talking.

"I just don't think it's a good idea, that's all," she said.

"Why not, Rayne?" Dad said. "Why not? I don't think Michael is the kind of kid that can adjust to something like that."

"I won't have him in my house. When we made our vows we said we would start a new life. We stressed the word *new*, Dick, remember?"

"I just don't see how he will inter*fere*," Dad replied. "He's a great kid."

"He's irresponsible and he needs discipline. I thought it was just going to be us, Dick. *Us*. You remember that?"

"Yes, Rayne," Dad said, "I remember everything I said. But this might only be for a few months."

"Sure. Oh, sure. A few months turns into a few

years, and the next thing you know he'll be here forever, always leaving his basketball in the front closet. I don't want to be tripping over basketballs for the rest of my life, Dick. I won't have it. It's either him or me. I said I'd be willing to help out in any way, and you know Florence has a boy at that school. She said it's really helping him."

"I just don't think Michael needs that, Rayne. He's a *good kid*."

"A lot of *good kids* go there, Dick. It's a school for good kids. It's not a *prison*. You're such a sucker for *myths*."

I didn't want to hear any more. I quietly walked into the bathroom and shut the door. I didn't even go for a couple of minutes. I just sat on the toilet seat, in the dark, and cradled my face in my hands. I wanted to run away, but I didn't know where.

Eventually, I went to the bathroom and slouched back to the guest room. I thought about Alice, and how much I missed her. I pictured her doing the Charleston in the living room.

When I woke up, I felt like I'd gotten nailed in the stomach with a sledgehammer. My guts were in knots.

I walked down to the kitchen to try to shove something into my stomach. Dad had left a note on the counter. It read:

Dear Michael,

Rayne and I discussed everything last night and came up with a solution. Please pack up your stuff and be ready to go by 3:30. Don't forget your ball in the garage. Please be ready. I'm getting off work early for this. See you soon.

Love,
Dad

I read the note about four times. Each time, the words *Please pack up your stuff* got larger and larger. The note crumpled in my brain and stuck there like a piece of extra-strength flypaper. I remembered Dad and Rayne's muffled conversation. I remembered Rayne calling me irresponsible and undisciplined. I remembered something about Florence's son at some school. I thought I was going to swallow my tongue.

I went upstairs and started to pack. A lot of my clothes were dirty, but Consuela was really cool and washed them for me.

There's something really scary about folding your clothes and stuffing them in a suitcase when you don't know where you're going. It's like walking down a street that you've never seen before. All of the houses look so sad because there's nobody in them you know. Your underwear and socks suddenly become your best friends. You start doing a lot of sappy symbolic things, stroking your favorite shirt, pulling your sweatpants close, and offering your underwear reassurances that everything's going to be all right.

I started folding this purple sweatshirt Mom had bought me for a camping trip. I remembered how much it smelled like the woods when I came back.

I'd worn it every day and the sweet hickory scent of the campfire lingered on the collar for a long time. It didn't have anything fancy on the chest like spiderweb stitching or a picture of Ken Griffey, Jr., hitting a homer, but I liked it anyway. I guess it was kind of extra-special because it meant Mom had thought of me right before I left for the trip.

As I held it to my chest, I pictured her chucking all of Alice's loose change in a fountain and making a wish; a really great wish about me coming out to Boston and hooking up with the tour. I'd sort out all of Alice's fan mail and arrange her flowers, and there would be a basketball court behind the theater where Alice and I would play H.O.R.S.E., and I'd watch her flounce around and shoot granny style, and at night we'd sneak down to the restaurant after it closed, and she would play me "Chopsticks" on the piano, or sing "Castle on a Cloud," and I would lie on the floor and let my mind go blank.

Dad came home at 3:15 with his tie all wrapped around his neck like he'd just run through a wind tunnel, like he was completely rushing and in a hurry.

"Hey, sport," he said. He never called me *sport*.

He sounded like a TV show. "You got all your stuff packed?"

"Where are we going?"

"You'll see, Mike, you'll see. Don't worry about that yet. Just get your suitcase and meet me out front. And don't forget your ball out of the garage." I just stood there frozen for a second. "Let's go! Chop, chop!" he said. "I have to be back at a reasonable hour."

"Where we going, Alaska?"

"Yeah, we're going to Anchorage. We're gonna put in a new pipeline," he said like a game show host. "Seriously, Mike, let's go. I'm on borrowed time here."

As I lugged my suitcase to the garage and collected my ball, I fantasized about Rayne tripping over it and spraining her neck. I saw myself planting a bunch of balls all over their house; soccer balls in the bathroom under her vanity, footballs in every corner, and about three basketballs in the front closet. I'd even stick a couple of softballs under her pillow. She'd live a life of lumpy pillow headaches and broken ankles and I would jump for joy.

In the car, Dad quickly turned the radio on, probably to ward off any possibility of a conversation.

He listens to this really half-baked station with Linda Ronstadt and Elton John and a bunch of other old fartbags.

I'm into hip-hop and funk. I basically like anything you can dance to, even though I'm not what you'd exactly call the second coming of Marky Mark.

I switched the station to WGCI. Dad and I didn't say anything to each other, just sat there letting an Afro Sheen commercial wash over us. I reached over and increased the volume of the radio.

"You really like this stuff, huh?" he asked.

"What?" I said, "Sportin' Waves?"

"This music."

I didn't say anything. I turned the station to one of those easy-listening, senior citizen, crossword puzzle stations. Andy Williams was singing a song. I wondered where Dad was taking me. Every so often, I'd glance over at him to see if he looked like he might say something, but he was silent.

I watched all of the road signs whiz by like streaks of green. I saw a sign that read "Racine 24." The only Racine I'd ever heard of was Racine, Wisconsin, where Mom mail-orders for all her gourmet cheese.

"Dad," I said, "where are you taking me?"

He didn't answer.

"I just saw a sign back there for Racine, Wisconsin," I said.

He still said nothing.

"What's goin' on, Dad? Are you gonna drop me off at a cheese factory or something?"

"No, Mike. No, I'm not gonna drop you off at a *cheese* factory." He ran his hands through his hair and started shifting his weight.

"Well, what? Jesus, Dad, can you tell me, please? I think I have a right to know. I mean, you write me this *stupid* note about packing and crap and I don't even know where the hell I'm going."

"Calm down, Michael. Don't talk to me like that. I'm your father. Just calm down."

He looked over at me a couple of times before he said anything else, like he wanted to make sure the door was locked so I couldn't jump out.

"Michael," he said, "I'm taking you to a school where you can stay. A boarding school."

"A what?"

"A boarding school, where you live and learn and make all kinds of great friends. It's a military academy."

"A *what* academy?"

"A military academy. It's like a regular school, only you live there and it has a lot of structure. They have a great basketball program, too. All of their sports are fantastic. It's a great school. Rayne's friend, Florence, has a kid there. He really likes it."

I didn't say anything. I just felt my jaw freeze shut, and my eyes try to pop themselves out of my head. I was totally deranged. I thought I would lose it all over the crushed velvet interior of his Cadillac. One minute, you're playing H.O.R.S.E. in your backyard and before you know it you're off to military school, just like that.

"It's the best thing for everyone right now," he said. "Rayne and I feel that this is a great opportunity for a kid like you."

"Yeah," I said, "for a kid who steals cars and breaks windows and needs discipline and all of that crap."

"No, son, that's not what kind of school it is."

"Dad, a kid in my social studies class was sent to a boarding school after he punched out Mr. Gentry, the guidance counselor."

"It's not a school like that, Michael. A bunch of really great kids go there. *The cream of the crop.* They don't try to make soldiers out of you, they just use the structure to teach self-discipline and leadership tools and stuff. College prep stuff. To get the best out of you. Besides, a little discipline never hurt anyone. A little structure does a person good. I wish I could've had this opportunity when I was your age. These kinds of things don't come around very often, Michael."

"Why can't I just stay with you and Rayne? I'll go to school in the city. I don't care."

"No, Michael. I wish that could happen, I really do. But it can't. It's just not going to work. Rayne and I both have careers and it would be too much for us to have to watch over you all the time."

"Please, Dad," I said. "Let me stay with you. I won't get in the way, I promise. I'll keep my basketball in the garage and I'll get discipline. I don't want to march around and spin rifles and crap. I'll go *buy* some discipline if I have to. Please, Dad. I don't want to go to any school where you have to be structured. I'll structure myself. I promise, I swear. I don't want to wear a uniform. I don't want to look like Colonel Sanders. Please let me stay with you, Dad."

"I know you don't want to go, son, but this is the best thing for you right now. You'll see. It's the best thing for all of us." I started bawling. I couldn't help it.

"C'mon, sport, don't cry," Dad said. "You gotta be a man about this. This is a man's world. You'll be fine. Just relax."

He started petting my hair with his free hand. It felt kind of nice, even though I hated his guts for letting Rayne push him around, even though he was a complete bastard.

"Just relax, Mike. Everything's gonna work out."

He reached into the backseat and handed me a bunch of purple-and-red folders.

"Check this stuff out," he said. "There's a lot of really neat stuff in there. I think there's even some information about the athletic program. I think they have something like twenty-seven sports. Alpine skiing and the whole bit."

The first folder had "St. Matthew's Military Academy" written across the top, and "Where Boys Become Men" along the bottom. I pictured a zillion kids my age running through the woods with fatigue uniforms and painted faces, beating the crap out of each other with bamboo sticks. I thought of one of those Army recruiting commercials where all of the guys have expensive haircuts and look like their names are Lance.

I opened it up to find the word "P.O.T.E.N.T.I.A.L." stamped down the left margin. A corresponding word was attached to every letter: Pride for P, Order for O, Toughness for T, and so on.

There was a picture of a kid in a parade uniform

who looked like he was twenty-eight years old. He wore this black, cylindrical helmet with a giant plume sticking out the top. He had all of these brass buttons popping off of his chest, and he was holding a sword, like he was in the Civil War or something. The caption read: "1st Lieutenant Jim Baker enrolled as a recruit and graduated as an officer!"

There was another picture on the next page of this lanky guy slam dunking a basketball. His hair looked like sandpaper, and he had this terrible grimace on his face like he had gas backed up in his intestines.

"So, whaddya think?" Dad asked. "You see anything you like?"

"No," I replied, looking out the window.

"C'mon, sport, whaddya think?"

"Looks like it's a place where everyone gets brainwashed and watches old war movies. Like Uncle Sam might swoop down in a helicopter and start throwing candy."

"Did you read the stuff on the sports?"

"No."

"Did you at least look at the pictures?"

"Yeah," I said. "This guy who's slam dunking looks like a girl at our school we called the Flying

Hooka Monster. Completely half-baked, if you ask me. It looks like the place is full of a bunch of spastic, G.I. Joe pansies."

"Oh, Michael, you're always such a joker about everything. I can understand that, though. It's part of growing up. You gotta make jokes about everything." He shook his head a couple of times. "I'm glad you have a good sense of humor," he said. "You and your sister both."

I threw all the literature in the back seat and wedged my head between my seat belt and the window. I watched the steam from my mouth evaporate on the window by my cheek. My breathing became very deep and slow. I thought about how doomed I was, how in a few hours I'd be running through the woods with bamboo sticks, getting the crap beat out of me. I thought about becoming a man and getting my hair buzzed off and all of that. I felt like a tremendous clothing bag full of old bones.

My lids became very heavy, and I started to lean harder against the seat. Some old fartbag was singing "My Way" on the radio.

chapter four

Wishing for the Silent Helicopter

When I woke up, we were passing through this little town called Oakfield, population 3,500. All of the houses looked really sad, with broken tricycles and iron dog figurines and skeletons of abandoned cars littering their yards. It was one of those towns that looked like it was trapped in a time warp, like it was still 1955, and everyone should have had twenty-foot Chevies.

There was a barbershop with one of those candy-striped tubes that spins forever, next to a church that had a flaking coat of white paint. It was the kind of place I always had envisioned Tom Sawyer and Huckleberry Finn playing pirates and chasing Becky Thatcher around.

Dad stayed on the street with the barbershop

and the white church for about a mile, and then made a left by a bunch of pine trees. There was this huge, black, iron arch with "St. Matthew's Military Academy" stamped in calligraphic letters across the top. In a distant green field I could see a bunch of kids dressed like marines, flipping rifles around and marching. Dad made a left, and the whole place suddenly appeared, seemingly out of nowhere. There were a zillion trees with different-colored leaves spread out over the whole campus. I'd never seen so many different-colored leaves in my life.

All of the buildings were made out of granite rocks and resembled little castles, with lookout towers and the whole bit. The grounds looked the way I'd always imagined King Arthur's court, like at any second Sir Lancelot or someone with armor and chain mail would come galloping through, holding a lance. Dad parked the car.

"Well," he said, "this is it." He stretched his legs and yawned a couple of times. "Is it what you expected?"

"Looks like feudalism or something," I said. I really didn't know what feudalism was, but I remembered from social studies that feudal lords had castles and drawbridges.

"It's great, isn't it?" Dad said. I didn't answer.

We walked toward a building with "Spalding Hall" engraved above the entrance. I heard a bunch of faint commands in the distance where a platoon of kids was marching on this huge lot of asphalt. I could see them pivoting in synchronization. Dad opened the door to Spalding Hall and we walked in.

A long, glossy, marble hallway extended for what seemed hundreds of feet. There were a couple of retired-looking old men in green uniforms walking around with papers in their hands, and a fat secretary darting from office to office.

On the wall to my left hung a glass display case the size of a billboard, full of a zillion medals. They all stood for something different. Some of them had these weird military names like the Military Training III Leadership Award, and others were more academic, like the English I Strotzcliffe Award.

"Pretty neat, huh?" Dad beamed, touching the display. I didn't say anything.

"Mr. Tegroff?" I heard the sound of a man's voice as I stared at my reflection in the case of medals. I looked like a fading ghost.

"I'm Dr. Sharifporte. I spoke with you earlier this morning. Pleased to meet you."

"Oh, how are you, Dr. Sharifporte. So that was you?" Dad said. "Great."

I turned around and saw one of those men in the green uniforms shaking hands with Dad. He had all of these ribbons pinned on his chest and a bunch of chevrons stacked on his shoulder. "You must be Michael," he said. "Can I call you Mike?"

"Yeah," I said. "Sure." He extended his hand and we shook.

"I'm Dr. Sharifporte, director of admissions here at St. Matthew's."

He had one of those handshakes that makes you grit your teeth so hard the plaque falls off. Dad always told me to have a firm grip whenever I shook hands with a man because it's a sign of confidence. I felt about as confident as an epileptic in a strobe-lit disco.

Dr. Sharifporte smiled the whole time we shook. There's nothing phonier than a guy you've never met before, in a green uniform with a bunch of ribbons, acting like he's your best friend.

"I've heard a lot about you," he said, releasing my hand from his kung fu grip. "I'm glad you could make it." I flashed a smile at him and looked at Dad.

"Shall we get started?" Dr. Sharifporte said, and directed us to his office, which was down the blue hallway. It was next to a portrait of this old priest with knives for eyebrows who looked haunted.

"So," Dr. Sharifporte said, "your father tells me you're quite a basketball player." I didn't respond and just walked along. "We have a new junior varsity coach this year. Mr. Savery. I'll introduce you to him later."

I've only been on campus for ten minutes, and this guy with a bad mustache is programming my life, I thought.

When we got to his office, Dad and I sat down in front of Dr. Sharifporte's desk. I checked out the room while he started talking. I tried to tune him out, but I caught a couple of phrases about how St. Matthew's would *catalyze the search for your potential* and help *you be all you can be* and other malarkey, like something you'd hear on TV. It was quite a sales pitch. I thought he was going to throw in a set of Japanese knives.

After I shook the sand out of my left foot, which had fallen asleep in the office, Dr. Sharifporte gave us a tour of the campus. All of the stony buildings seemed to angle in, like they were stalking me. In the distance I could see these really old lead cannons. Dr. Sharifporte said they were actual relics from the Civil War. Dad seemed really impressed with everything.

Then Dr. Sharifporte took us to the field house, which had all of these shadowy entrances and looked like it was loaded with trapdoors. Dr. Sharifporte pointed out the new break-away rims, which he called *goals* like they called them back in the fifties. He said something about how great the basketball team was supposed to be.

After that he showed us the barracks, the baseball diamond, the football stadium, the soccer field, the library, the school buildings, the academy infirmary, and the newly molded, purple-and-red tennis courts.

Finally, Dr. Sharifporte took us down a bunch of stairs to a little shop he called the cadet store. It was dimly lit and resembled the waiting room of a dentist's office. Two very old Asian women began fitting me for all of my uniforms. They didn't even stop to say hi or ask me my name or anything, they just plastered me with a bunch of measuring tapes and safety pins and rulers, like they were programmed or had a couple of Duracell batteries stuck in their backs.

Every so often they'd say something in their mystery language and laugh, like they were telling jokes about how deranged my dimensions are. My legs are almost twice as long as my upper body, and my arms are lanky, too. I'm pretty tall for a freshman; about five-ten. I guess I don't look very symmetrical.

There were a zillion uniforms: one for classes, with these navy blue stripes down the sides; one for parades, which required you to wear that goofy hat with the plume and all of those brass buttons; one for church, which came with a tie and a sport coat; one for drill, which was fatigue-colored; and one for police duty, a set of overalls like the ones mechanics wear. The two Asian women called them coveralls. I felt like I was modeling for G.I. Joe's wedding reception.

When they said *police duty*, I pictured myself getting arrested and forced into a single-file line, where I'd be beaten with a bamboo stick until I could say the Army alphabet backwards.

Dr. Sharifporte and Dad entertained themselves talking about the Nixon years or whatever had them so fascinated with each other. They sounded like a couple of really bad clarinets tooting out the history of the world.

I also was issued a bunch of supplies I'd need for the entire semester. Black shoe polish, cotton balls, toothpaste, envelopes, sheets, shampoo, soap, and stuff like that.

There was a mechanical hum purring out of this mysterious back room. I envisioned tiny elves dressed in little green military uniforms slaving away at sewing machines. I thought maybe they also knew about me. Maybe *they* had big plans for me, too.

Following our shopping spree at the cadet store, Dr. Sharifporte led us to the barracks, where he escorted us to my new room. He opened the oak doors to one of those castle-like buildings called Glenwood Hall. As we heaved my new footlocker up four flights of brick stairs, I was completely silent and kind of scared. I knew absolutely nothing about rifles, or uniforms, or cleaning brass, or shining shoes. In fact, I'm completely retarded when it comes to those kinds of things. There are times when I have a problem *tying* my shoes, let alone *shining* them.

When we reached the fourth floor, Dr. Sharifporte directed us to my room. It looked like a glorified cell: four walls, a couple of closets, and this cheap carpeting that looked like it was ripped off the top of a pool table. A steel bunk bed stood in the right corner, and opposite that a porcelain sink hung below a mirrored medicine chest. At the end of the room were two desks with three drawers each, and one window that gave a view of the parking lot.

I looked out and could see Dad's Cadillac. I fantasized about grabbing the keys out of his pocket and making a dash for the car, outwitting Dr. Sharifporte, the military police, and everyone else at the school. But where would I go? I couldn't go back to Dad's house, and Mom was in Boston, or Philadelphia, or wherever the hell she was, and I didn't have enough money for a hotel. I thought I'd just drive, and drive, and drive, anywhere, as long as I was on an open highway that kept going.

"Where's everybody else?" Dad asked, while checking out the closet space.

"Oh. They're all out on the New Boy Drill Field preparing for Company Competitions. In a few minutes they'll be marching in for third mess." Dr. Sharifporte always had to look directly into your eyes when he said something.

All of the lingo was pretty scary. I didn't even know what a company was. It was like he was speaking some kind of verbal Morse Code.

After we "situated" my room, Dr. Sharifporte patted me on the back.

"Well, guess what, soldier?" he said. "You're the

only active new boy on the campus who has his own room. You're already starting out with *privileges*." Yes, that was my freshly appointed title—a *new* boy—like I was the second coming of Baby New Year. I just smiled again and looked at Dad. He was grinning as if he'd just bought a new set of whitewalls for his Cadillac.

"After third mess," Dr. Sharifporte said as he flicked some lint off his lapel, "you'll have to complete a series of entrance examinations. Some simple math and vocabulary words. Nothing too difficult. You should have no problem. Your father says you're a pretty good student." They smiled at each other like they were on a TV show. I felt my face heating up again.

"After the tests, your dad will be free to leave."

"Well, Dr. Sharifporte," Dad said, "unless it's absolutely necessary, I think I'd better get going pretty shortly. I have a long trip and I have to be back at a reasonable hour. My wife's expecting me."

"Oh well, that's fine," Dr. Sharifporte replied, happier than ever. I thought even his mustache was smiling. "Whatever's convenient," he added.

Dr. Sharifporte led us out of the room and back to the stairwell. A couple of marching drums thundered. It sounded like the theme song to

Hogan's Heroes. A giant window overlooked the campus. The panes of glass were vibrating.

"Here they come," Dr. Sharifporte said, standing up a little straighter, like he was about to salute Colonel Sanders or something.

"Look there, Mike," Dad said. "That's some pretty fancy dancin', huh?" He was talking about the parade that suddenly had appeared below us.

"They're marching in for third mess," Dr. Sharifporte said, with a sort of star-spangled twinkle in his eye. He was so excited about the whole ordeal I thought he was going to start singing "Oh, When the Saints Go Marching In."

The drums got louder and louder, and I heard a voice barking "Left, left, left-right-left-right, left." It sounded like some kind of fancy funeral procession, and I felt like the one who had died.

I stared out the window, over the campus, out to the horizon that was bleeding all sorts of colors into the tops of trees. I focused on the orange near the sun and how it kind of changed to lavender and this other purplish color that hasn't even been named yet. I tried to imagine a place where I could be alone and think about things. I pictured a kind of mountaintop, with a lot of clouds and grass, and a couple of goats, and other things that belong on the tops of mountains. I saw a gigantic grand piano there, too, looking all black and classical, and then Alice suddenly appeared, and her gray eyes got all mixed in with the clouds that were blowing around. She sat down and flipped the lid of the piano keys, and I lay down in the grass and petted one of the goats, and then she started playing "Chopsticks," a really nice version of it, and it was really slow and sad. Then I closed my eyes and let my head go clear, and the wind blew the etherlight clouds through my hair and the goat *baa*ed. Everything felt like home again.

I felt Dad's hand on the back of my neck. All of the drums had hushed and the last of the marching had vanished.

"Are you hungry, Mike?" Dr. Sharifporte asked in a soft voice. "Swedish meatballs or pork chops? It's your choice." I nodded my head.

Dad patted the back of my neck real soft. "Well, Michael," he said, "I better get going. I have a long day tomorrow, and it's already sunset. Rayne doesn't like me driving when it's dark."

"I know, Dad." I just kept staring out the window, wishing for a silent helicopter to rescue me and take me to my mountaintop.

□ □ □

I walked with Dad out to his car to get my suitcase and basketball. Dr. Sharifporte stayed about fifty feet behind us. I guess that meant I was supposed to be alone with Dad so we could say good-bye.

Dad was walking kind of fast and kept nervously fiddling with his crotch.

"So, do you think you can manage this?"

"I don't know," I said. He wouldn't look at me. "I guess I don't have a choice."

"Just remember, Mike, this is the best thing for *all of us*. I think you'll get a lot out of it. Just give it a try and keep an open mind." At this point, my mind was completely closed and welded shut with iron rivets.

"Yeah, Dad," I said as he opened the trunk and handed me my suitcase and ball, "an open mind. Whatever."

My face started heating up again, and I felt like I was about to get a really bad case of diarrhea.

I wanted him to turn and look at me. I wanted Dad to turn his head and at least catch a glimpse of me. I wanted him to see how I was walking, how terrible my posture was. I wanted him to wonder why my face was all red and heated up. And I wanted him to say something else besides the crap about "keeping an open mind," anything besides that. I wanted him to look me in the eyes and fluff my hair and tell me everything would be all right.

I guess I wanted him to say *I love you, Michael*. I guess I wanted to hear that more than anything.

He just stood there and looked away.

"Hang in there, son," he said. "Keep your head up."

He softly punched me in the shoulder and turned to get in his Cadillac.

"I'll keep in touch," he said. I nodded and watched him lower his head under the roof of the car. He backed out of the parking lot, flipped the lights on, and rode off. His Cadillac became smaller and smaller, and then disappeared under the black arch, just like a magic trick.

I slowly turned around, fixed my ball under my arm, and grabbed my suitcase. Dr. Sharifporte came kind of close and said, "C'mon, Mike. Let's go eat. We have a lot to talk about." He took my suitcase, and together we entered Spalding Hall.

chapter five

Gee, I'm a Tree

That night, after eating what looked like balls of dog food and rubber shoelaces (Swedish meatballs), I took those tests Dr. Sharifporte talked about. I swear, one of Jerry's Kids could have aced them. They were so easy I almost was tempted to mess up on purpose, so they'd stick me in the infirmary for a couple of weeks to examine the fluid in my brain.

There was this one math problem: If James has five nickels and he throws two into a fountain, how much money will he end up with? I couldn't believe it. I wrote "not enough" next to the little dot that coincided with fifteen cents.

The whole ordeal lasted a couple of hours, and my butt cheeks cramped up from all the sitting and waiting around. When I finished the last vocabulary test, Dr. Sharifporte escorted me to the campus barber. He left me there and told me to report to his office to pick up my class schedule when I was done.

The barber was this really ugly man who looked like he'd murdered his family. He was close to seven feet tall, had about three hairs on his head, and these terrifically gruesome buck teeth that were all over the place. He also had a wandering eye. I couldn't tell which one he was looking at me with.

"C'mon, stholdier, jump on up," he lisped. There was this huge pile of hair beneath my feet. It was really gross. I could see ticks and dandruff and scalp boogers all tangled in the mess.

"Your firtht time?" he asked, cloaking me with a smock and practically strangling me with this piece of hard tissue he slung around my neck.

"Yeah. First time," I said.

"Then you get the thpethal."

He snapped my head back and turned on this violent razor that looked like some kind of torture device or machine from a funeral home. When it clicked on it made this really annoying buzzing noise that practically rattled my spine.

"Where you from?" he asked, driving the razor

through my hair, mowing everything right off.

"Chicago," I replied. I like to tell people I'm from Chicago, even though I live twenty-five minutes away.

"Oh. Another windy thity boy. We got a lotta them around here." The razor was whining like a chain saw. My head started to get cold.

"Your parenths drop you off today?"

"No," I said. "Just my dad."

"How do you like it tho far?"

"Oh. It's okay. I guess."

"You'll get uthed to it."

He clicked the razor off and turned on this vacuum hose and moved it all around my scalp and neck, and down my shirt.

Then he whirled me around so I could catch a glimpse of myself in the mirror. I was completely shocked. You think you have a pretty good idea of who you are because you watch yourself in the mirror when you brush your teeth and pop pimples. I know it all sounds pretty gross, but it's true. You get to know yourself through all that personal stuff.

With all the time I'd spent with myself, I never thought I had the potential to look like an acorn. Yes, that's what I looked like—an *acorn*. All my hair was shaved off the ears and collar, and I was left with a little tuft on top. I thought maybe I'd turn into an oak tree when I took a shower or something.

"Whaddya think? Thort huh?"

"Yeah," I said. "Pretty short." I looked at the barber smiling at me in the mirror. One of his eyes was checking out my reaction and the other was wandering all over the place.

I could see my scalp. I looked like I was on chemotherapy.

The barber released me from the smock, brushed off the chair and smiled.

"Look at all that hair," he said. "No hippieths around here." His buck teeth had kind of a blue tint, as if he'd just gnawed on a Smurf in the back room. I just smiled and walked toward the door, fearing a set of beaver teeth sinking into the back of my neck.

"Take it eathy," he said, sweeping his new batch of hair toward the pile.

"Yeah. Take it easy," I said, walking out the door, feeling like I'd escaped something terrible.

When I returned to Dr. Sharifporte's office, he was talking to a man I hadn't seen before. The new guy looked kind of young, about twenty-five. He had an Elvis Presley hairdo and was wearing a purple-

and-red sweatsuit that had "Lancers" written in cursive script across the front. They were both looming over a couple of file folders, nodding their heads. When I appeared at the door, Dr. Sharifporte quickly plastered a smile all over his face, like the cameras were rolling again and someone had yelled "action."

"Hey there, Mr. Tegroff," Dr. Sharifporte said. "Look at you. How 'bout that," he said, staring at my head. "Clean cut and ready to go."

"I think he took a little too much off the sides," I replied, thumbing at the cold space above my ears.

"Oh, don't worry. You'll get used to it. You'll feel like your old self in a couple of days."

Dr. Sharifporte closed the file folders and bolstered his posture so he looked like an erection.

"Mike," he said, "I'd like you to meet someone who I think you'll be very interested in. This is Mr. Savery, the new junior varsity basketball coach." Dr. Sharifporte turned to the other man and pointed his hand toward me with an open palm. "Mr. Savery, this is Michael Tegroff. Prospective Lancer basketball star."

Mr. Savery stuck out his hand and we shook. His grip was a lot friendlier than Dr. Sharifporte's.

"Hi, Mike," Mr. Savery said. "Nice to meet you.

Where you from?"

"Chicago," I said.

"Oh. Another Chicago boy." What was it with all of the Chicago boys? I thought. There were probably a lot of kids in Chicago whose dads were married to rich bimbos like Rayne. "Looks like I'm gonna have you in my English class." I nodded.

"What position do you play?" he asked.

"Point guard. But I can play a little off guard too. I've been working hard on my shooting range. Close to twenty feet."

"Well, that's good to hear. We need as many hard workers as we can get our hands on."

I don't think he was very impressed with me.

"I look forward to having you as a student-athlete," he continued. "If you need anything, let me know. I live on the third floor of Spalding."

"Thanks," I said.

"I'll see you in class." Mr. Savery smiled, shook my hand again, and walked out of the office with a file folder.

"Well," Dr. Sharifporte said, "you're all ready to go. We figured out your schedule based on your test scores. You did very well. Here's your schedule."

He handed me a piece of paper with my classes on it.

"Tomorrow, you'll need to go back to the cadet store after lunch and pick up your books. They'll hand you a voucher. You'll have to show it to your teachers."

I put the paper in my pocket.

"Your uniforms have all been tailored and delivered to your room. The next step is for you to go back to the barracks and get familiar with everything. You're about two weeks behind all of the other new cadets, so you're gonna have to learn quickly, but you're obviously a smart young man and I don't think you'll have a problem." The whole time he talked, he didn't blink, and he kind of smiled. He looked like he was modeling for a wax museum. "One thing we do here in order to help cadets make the adjustment of being away from home for the first time is put off telephone privileges for six weeks."

"So I can't use the phone for *six weeks*?"

"It's a policy that applies to all new cadets. It's not a punishment. It will help you adjust to things a little faster, that's all."

When I left his office, I walked back to Glenwood Hall. On the way, I stopped to look at this huge statue that was made out of round rocks. It was shaped like a giant cone and had this fake flame flickering at the top. There were a bunch of wilting sunflowers planted all around its base. On each side of the statue hung a copper plaque with an engraved phrase. One said "Work Hard," another said "Play Hard," another said "Pray Hard," and the final one said "Don't Be a Mollycoddle." A *mollycoddle*?

These three kids in gym shorts and white T-shirts walked by me and saluted the statue. At first, I thought they were saluting me, but then I realized they couldn't see me because I was kind of hiding behind all of the rocks. What a bunch of fools, I thought. Who in their right mind would salute a bunch of rocks?

About fifty feet off in the distance, toward the Civil War cannons, a kid was marching under floodlights all by himself on this pond of asphalt. He was carrying a rifle. He'd walk about twenty yards, stop, boost the rifle off his shoulder so it would land next to his feet, spin his body around, jackknife the rifle back up to his shoulder, and walk twenty yards in the opposite direction. I watched him for about two minutes. He looked really lonely, I thought, and he had this really sad expression on his face. He looked like the ghost of a kid who'd blown his brains out.

chapter six

The Comfort of Arms

I turned out of the stairwell and peered down the corridor. There were a couple of kids wearing those blue coveralls walking on the right side of the hall, next to the wall. They had black shoes in their hands. My room was all the way down the hall, in the corner. I walked really slow, fearing that if I walked too fast someone would jump out of a corner and beat me with a bamboo stick. All of the doors were open. I tried not to look in anybody's room, but out of the corner of my eye, I could see some kids sitting at their desks, shining their black shoes.

When I reached my room, I pulled my schedule out of my pocket and sat down at my desk. I had a lot of classes: Algebra I, M.T. I, Physical Education, Biology, English I, U.S. History, and

Spanish I. I heard a knock at my door. I looked up. A humongous fat kid with a fake tan was standing in my doorway, holding a clipboard. There's nothing dumber than a fat kid with a fake tan. Something about it just doesn't look right. It's like a nun who wears designer jeans.

"You Tegroff?"

"Yeah," I said.

"It's *Yes, sir.* Let's try it again." He disappeared for a second and came back. "You Tegroff?"

"Yeah, sir."

"It's yes, sir. *Yes*, sir, not *yeah*, sir." He had the kind of voice that sounded like it was underwater, like his blubber was smothering his lungs.

"Yes, sir," I said.

"Good," he said. "I'm Staff Sergeant Hillcrest, your new squad leader. Welcome to Delta Company."

"Thanks. Nice to meet you," I said.

"You're two weeks behind. You gotta helluva lot to learn. The first thing you need to learn is that whenever a cadet enters your room, you *immediately* snap to attention."

"What's that?"

"It means you stand up tall as a dick, flex your arms at your sides, fix your heels together with your feet forty-five degrees apart, and stare straight ahead. Try it."

"Now?" I asked.

"Yeah, now!" he barked. I stood up and tried to mimic what he said. He pinched my fingers together at my sides and kicked my feet apart more. When he came close I could smell his breath. It smelled like he'd just finished eating somebody's dead dog.

"That's right," he said. "You are to assume this position until the entering cadet tells you to stand *at ease*. Then you can sit down. Got it?"

"Yeah," I said, feeling my knees shaking.

"What?"

"Yes, sir."

"Say it like you mean it, Tegroff!"

"Yes, sir!" I screamed.

"OK. At ease."

Hillcrest went over to the other desk, dropped his clipboard, and sat down. "Where you from?" he asked.

"Chicago."

"Oh. Another F.I.B."

"What's an F.I.B.?" I asked.

"A Fucking Illinois Bastard."

"Oh," I said, trying to hide my shaking knees.

"Where are you from?" I asked.

"Florida," he said. "But that's N.F.B. to you."

"What's N.F.B.?"

"*None of your fucking business,* that's what it is! I ask the questions here." Just what I needed, I thought: a blimp with an attitude.

"Why are you starting so fucking late?" he asked, shuffling his fat hands through my desk drawers.

"I don't know. I didn't even know I was coming here till today."

"Well, Tegroff, you aren't at mommy's house anymore. You can't come home from school and turn on *Scooby Doo.* No one around here's gonna clean up your spilled milk. You are now what is referred to as a *new boy.* Basically, that means you're the lowest scum on the totem pole. It means everyone around here is sir to you. It means that Little Jack Crappypants can kick the shit out-taya if he wants to."

"Who's Little Jack Crappypants?"

"*Anyone,* Tegroff. Anyone who has one of these stripes on his shoulder." He pointed to the side of his arm, where all of these dramatic chevrons were. "He runs my shit house and only comes outside when he gets really mad. Do you understand?"

"Yes, sir."

"Good. Now the first thing I'm gonna teach you is how to shine your shoes because we have a command reveille tomorrow."

"What's that?" I asked.

"You mean *sir*, what's that, right?" he said.

"Yes, sir."

"That means that at oh six hundred hours tomorrow morning you are going to be inspected by a staff officer. That means your uniform has to be perfect, and part of your uniform is your low-quarter shoes."

"Sir," I said, "what are my low-quarter shoes?"

"Your low-quarter shoes. Your *black shoes*. You have to *shine* them, and they have to be so shiny that if I look into them and smile, I will be able to see the corn in between my teeth. They're over there in your closet. Go get 'em."

"Yes, sir." I scurried over to my closet and pulled out my low-top black shoes. They looked like the kind of shoes inmates have to wear in prison; no fancy stitching or anything. While I was shuffling through my closet, which Hillcrest seemed to know more about than me, he was rooting through my footlocker with his fat hands. When I came out with the shoes, he was walking back to my desk with a box of cotton balls and a tin of black shoe polish.

"Here," he said. "Fill this with water." He handed me the top of the shoe polish tin. I cranked on the faucet, filled it with water, and brought it back to him where he was sitting at my desk. "You always want to moisten the cotton ball. If it's too wet, squeeze some water out. You need to form a base because these shoes are new." He filled the head of the soaked cotton ball with black wax and started polishing my shoes with little circular motions. "Always make reverse zero movements to get the best luster." Everything he said sounded like it was memorized from a manual, like a computer chip was stuck up his ass.

"Can you do this, Tegroff?"

"Yes, sir," I said.

"Good. I don't care if it takes you all night. You better have these polished like glass by oh six hundred tomorrow morning. Do you shave?" he asked.

"No, sir."

"Good, that's one less thing I have to worry about." I grabbed my black shoes and started polishing them. The wax was going on kind of rough. It didn't look like they had the potential to cast a reflection. They looked kind of gray and dingy, actually, like the surface of charcoal.

Hillcrest grabbed his clipboard and started going down this checklist.

"Your door will always stay open, unless I or someone above me closes it. Your sink and medicine chest should sparkle at all times. Use Comet and glass cleaner for that. Your garbage can should never have anything stuck to the sides. You will *never* chew gum or tobacco. Your bed will always be made in ten-ten fashion. I'll show you what that means later. If you need a vacuum to clean the carpet, contact me, my room is three doors down, to the left. If you're ever caught stealing, cheating, in possession of alcohol, you will be subject to suspension. If you are ever, at any time, caught in possession of marijuana or any other drugs, you will be dismissed from the academy immediately, with no refund of your tuition. Do you understand all of that, Tegroff?"

"Yes, sir," I said.

"Oh yeah," he said after all of that, "if you're ever caught runnin' for Old Shirley, you'll have enough guard path to give you nightmares about asphalt."

"Sir, who's Old Shirley?" I asked.

"The Fence. She's the mistress of your AWOL blues. Any more questions?"

"No, sir."

"Good. Put the shoes down, you can finish that later. I have to show you how to make your bed." He went back to my footlocker and grabbed some sheets and pillowcases, and then went into my closet and grabbed a blue comforter. He showed me how to make my bed, with a ten-inch collar and a ten-inch fold. The blue comforter had "St. Matthew's Military Academy" encircled in the center. He showed me how to make hospital corners and pull everything tight. I couldn't believe I had to do all of this just to go to sleep. With all the weird dreams I have, I'd probably just tear it all up anyway, I thought.

After that, Sergeant Hillcrest explained some of my uniforms to me, gave me the lowdown on the rest of the military stuff, and then he finally turned to leave.

"Get those shoes shined or I'll put you through the meat grinder. Don't get on my bad side, Tegroff. You don't want to do that."

"Yes, sir."

While he disappeared from my room, I saw myself harpooning him right in his fat stomach.

It was pretty late. I didn't even know what time it was. I looked out the window and realized how black it was outside. Everything seemed darker than usual. Even the moon had a grayer tint than normal. I heard a church bell in the distance. It gonged ten times. Someone stuck a hand in my doorway and flicked my light off.

Then, over the loudspeaker that was just outside my room, a bugle started playing really slow. I could tell it was an old recording because of all the static. It was taps. It made me feel kind of sad. I was sitting there at my desk, in the dark, staring at my shoes, holding a tin of black shoe polish, listening to taps. I soaked a cotton ball with water, rubbed it in the polish, and started making reverse zeros on the tip of my shoe. No one ever said anything about command reveilles, I thought. No one ever said anything about a huge, fat bastard threatening me with meat grinders.

My stomach knotted up again, and my throat started to get thick. I felt all hot and spooky inside. I thought about Dad and Rayne in that picture, wearing their cowboy outfits, on top of that horse, and I thought about Mom and Alice traveling around the country with each other, staying in hotels, and collecting roses with water tips, and meeting guys like Grover the agent. I thought about all of that, and then I thought about how dark it was, how I was sitting all alone, shining my shoes with the lights off, and I started bawling. I couldn't help it. It just came out of me because of how dark I felt. I didn't even have to use any water with the cotton ball because my tears were good enough. I cried for a long time holding my shoes, making little reverse zeros over and over again.

After a while, I just set my shoes down and put my arms around myself. I know that sounds pretty stupid, but I sort of wanted to be held, and nobody was around, so I just kind of hugged myself, right there in the room, at my desk, in the dark. I rocked back and forth with my arms around my shoulders, telling myself everything would be all right.

Eventually, I moved over to my bed and eased myself down. I didn't even bother getting under the covers. I just curled up kind of tight, with my knees in my chest and my arms around my legs. I didn't even care about my low-quarter shoes or command reveille.

"**T**egroff, get your ass up!"

I jumped out of my bed and snapped to attention, forgetting to split my feet apart. Hillcrest practically smashed my toes with his fat clodhoppers. He had my shoes in his hands and he was smacking the soles together. He was far too dramatic for five-thirty in the morning, with his uniform covering him like a set of humongous drapes and his hair slick from the shower. His face looked like a big, fat, tan bagel.

It was barely light out yet, and a bunch of birds were chirping outside my window.

"What the hell do you call this, Tegroff!?" he griped. He kept smacking the soles together. "What the fuck are you trying to *pull* here?"

"Sir," I said, standing as tall as my tired spine

would allow, looking straight ahead, "I don't know what you—"

"Don't give me that *bullshit*, you know exactly what I mean. You call these *shined*? You're going to actually stand here and tell me that these are *shined*, Tegroff?"

"I did my best, sir."

"Bullshit! I can't even see the cracks of my teeth."

"Sorry, sir."

"Drop and give me twenty-five."

I didn't know what the hell he was talking about. When he said "drop," I dropped down to my knees. He pulled me up by the back of my neck. "Twenty-five *push-ups*, you moron! You know what *push-ups* are?"

"Yes, sir."

"Well, give me twenty-five, and count off."

I dropped to my chest and started pumping off push-ups.

"No, you idiot! Like this."

He threw my shoes down, fell all over himself, and started doing push-ups, yelling *"One sir, two sir, three sir,"* and so on, until he reached six. I was shocked that the whale could even do three, let alone half a dozen.

He got up all hot and bothered, breathing like he'd just completed a fun run for fat people.

"Now drop, goddammit," he said in between breaths. There's nothing like waking up to a fat kid the size of Texas yelling at the top of his lungs. It makes you wonder why humans aren't arrested if they balloon over two hundred fifty pounds.

I dropped and pumped off the push-ups.

"Get up, Tegroff."

I stood at attention. I could feel my face heating up from all the push-ups.

"Welcome to my shit house," Hillcrest said. "Not too many people make it out. You just jumped on the wrong side of the fence, and you had better pray to God that your ass gets back on the other side, or you're gonna have one helluva miserable life in Delta Company." He started walking circles around me. "You see, Tegroff, there are these priceless little things called Silver M's. They're what all good new boys earn by Christmastime. For you, they're the road out of my shit house. Do you understand me?"

"Yes, sir!"

"Now if you don't have these looking like *ice* by six-fifteen, I'm gonna tear you a new asshole. Got it, Tegroff?"

71

"Yes, sir!"

"And don't even *think* about showering until after inspection. I don't want to see you outside this room. When I leave, I'd advise you to get knee-deep in polish. You understand me, Tegroff?"

"Yes, sir!"

When he left, I wiped the sleep from my eyes, collected my shoes that he'd completely scuffed, and started shining them, making little reverse zeros, wondering how to draw blood from a stone; or from a fat neck.

At six-fifteen Hillcrest reentered my room. I popped to attention and he quickly let me be at ease.

"Let's have 'em," he said. I handed him my shoes. He studied them, gritting his teeth over the tips, checking for a good reflection. "Well," he said, "they're better, but they're still not ice. You'll be lucky to pass inspection."

Some kid with a nasal voice started talking over the loudspeaker: *"Fifteen minutes first call command reveille, fifteen minutes first call command reveille. Uniform is class grays, sweaters, and low quarters. Fifteen minutes first call."*

"At ten minutes first call, I want you standing outside your room at parade rest. Like this." He spread his feet wide apart, about shoulder distance from each other, and folded his hands in the small of his back. "Can you do that, Tegroff?"

"Yes, sir." I tried to imitate what he did. He kicked my feet further apart and slapped my hands flat in the small of my back.

"Look front," he said. He went into my closet and pulled out my class gray uniform. "At ease. Put this on." He handed me my uniform and stepped back.

I changed into my light blue shirt and gray pants. Hillcrest watched me the whole time, like I was his fat girlfriend. He came kind of close and showed me how to fix my gig line, so the seam in my pants ran in line with my belt buckle and the seam in my shirt. I didn't like Hillcrest touching my waist.

"Now," he said, "when the inspecting officer presents himself in front of you, *when he clicks his heels together*, snap to attention as hard as you can and stare at his Adam's apple. When he pivots away from you, then go back to parade rest. Understand, Tegroff?"

"Yes, sir."

"You better not fuck this up, Tegroff. We pride ourselves on perfection here in Delta. That means if you fuck up, we fuck up, right?"

"Yes, sir."

□ □ □

At ten minutes first call, I stood at parade rest outside my room. Out of the corner of my eye, I could
see a couple of other kids standing in front of their
rooms, in the same position. I wanted to turn my
head to see them, to see if any of them looked like
they'd hardly slept and had acorn haircuts. Each
time I felt my head want to turn ever so slightly to
the right, I forced myself to look front, fearing
Hillcrest's breath on my neck.

At five minutes first call, I heard a bunch of
other kids filing out into the hallway. Some of them
were whispering and laughing under their breath. I
could see a couple of them who lived directly across
the hall in my field of vision. They were at parade
rest, but in a more relaxed version of it, leaning
against the wall and bobbing on their toes.

My legs started to get kind of tingly from all the
standing, and my underwear was kind of knifing
up my crack because I had to get dressed so fast.

Over the loudspeaker above my head, this bugle
started playing, and it sounded really old and sloppy
because of the static. When it was finished, someone yelled "Delta Company A-ten-*shun!*" I snapped
to attention, with my eyes fixed front and my feet
forty-five degrees apart. "Your command reveille

inspector is Cadet Captain Mark Bruck. Pa-rade
rest!" I flattened my hands in the small of my back
and spread my feet shoulder width apart. Time
seemed to pass very slowly. I listened to my breathing and I started zoning out. I forgot about my
underwear strangling my crack, and the fact that I
had to go to the bathroom, and my lackluster shoes,
and Hillcrest's ugly bagel face. I just thought about
a lot of cool empty space, and I put myself there, in
a Barcalounger with an iced tea in my hand, and
then Alice's voice came over a loudspeaker with
really good sound, without all of those staticky
bugles, and she sang one of her show tunes.

I thought about how much of a kick I get out of
Alice. Whenever she does anything, whether it's
vacuuming the living room or washing the silverware, she has to make a major production out of it.
I thought about the time Mom asked her to repot
a plant that fell off the piano. Alice grabbed a
bunch of garden supplies from the broom closet,
slipped on a pair of rubber gloves, fisted a couple
of mini-spades, flipped up the lid of the piano, and
started playing "Somewhere That's Green" from
Little Shop of Horrors, gloves and all, singing like a
miniature version of Liza Minnelli the whole time.

Then I thought about how at night, after Mom

would go to bed, we would sometimes sneak out to the living room, turn all the lights off, and just sit in front of the TV and watch a late show together. She would always sit about six inches away from the screen and I would have to pull her back by the coffee table so she wouldn't get TV poisoning. Even if the program was lousy it didn't matter. I thought about how nice it was just to sit there quietly in the dark with her and watch the blue light glow on her face.

A really loud click snapped directly in front of me. It was the inspecting officer. I popped to attention and stared at his Adam's apple. He wasn't exactly what I'd expected. I guess I expected a taller, fatter version of Hillcrest, with a more demented attitude. He was only a couple of inches taller than me.

Captain Bruck checked my gig line, made sure my back button was fastened, pinched the crease in my pants, and then stared down at my shoes. He studied them for about thirty seconds.

"You the new cadet?" he asked.

"Yes, sir," I said nervously, with a spastic quiver in my voice.

"Just got here yesterday, cadet?"

"Yes, sir."

"Outstanding shoes." I thought he was joking, I swear. "I'd give you a merit, but the sides aren't done. Excellent tips, though. When'd you start on 'em?"

"Last night, sir."

"Who taught you?"

"Sergeant Hillcrest, sir."

"He should be commended as well. Keep up the good work."

"Thank you, sir." Captain Bruck pivoted away and clicked his heels. I returned to parade rest, feeling like something very fat and heavy had been lifted from my chest.

At the end of the hall, someone shouted "Inspection's been completed!" Everyone went back in their rooms. I turned to go, but felt the shrill, underwater whine of Hillcrest's voice.

"Where the hell do you think you're going, Tegroff?"

"To my room, sir."

"Drop."

"Why, sir?"

"Drop, shithead!" he yelled in front of a bunch of kids who were still in the hallway, comparing shines.

I took the hint and fell to the floor, pumping out

pushups again, counting off the whole time.

"Get up!" he said after ten. My face heated up a zillion degrees. "Get in your room." I walked into my room and stood at attention. He kicked the doorstop, and slammed the door shut. "You know why I just dropped you, Tegroff?"

"No, sir," I replied, panting and heating up and all.

"Do you know what a *merit* is, Jackoff?"

"No, sir."

"Well, let me fill you in on a little clue, dumb-shit. It's what you get if you're a *good little boy* and your shoes are *nice and shiny*." He said that part all sing-songy like Mary Poppins. "And you didn't get one, did you, Jackoff?"

"No sir, but—"

"—BUT *SHIT!* If we don't win the inspection because of your *lack of merit*, I'm gonna pay a visit to my magic phone booth and turn into Little Jack Crappypants and kick the shit outtaya." He came real close again, like he wanted to French kiss or something. "You got that, Jackoff?"

"Yes, sir." I wanted to smear a tub of cream cheese all over his fat face. "Sir?"

"What!"

"Captain Bruck commended you on teaching

me to shine my shoes. He said if I would've spiffed up the sides, I would've gotten a merit."

"Fuck Bruck."

"Ten minutes first call first mess, ten minutes first call first mess, uniform is class grays, sweaters, and low quarters, formation is on the guard path, ten minutes first call."

"You better have your ass on the guard path at parade rest at five minutes first call, Tegroff. Here."

He opened my closet and threw a gray hat at me a zillion miles an hour. It hit me in the side of the head. It looked like something Smoky the Bear's illegitimate son would wear, shaped like a submarine sandwich, with a thin, red racing stripe streaking lengthwise across the middle. "I'd advise you to get going."

"Yes, sir."

The guard path was a big strip of asphalt that stretched for a few hundred feet. There was a flank of trees bisecting the middle, with sandstone benches sitting in the shade like huge fossils. Piles of leaves had collected under all of the trees.

There were at least three hundred kids all lined up in their companies like figures on a chessboard, behind these purple and red flags. Everyone was facing a huge stone building that looked like a church, with lavender and orange stained glass windows. A huge lawn connected the church and all of the companies like a green moat. A zillion birds were chirping.

Hillcrest was already out there, pacing back and forth in front of his squad.

"Over here, Jackoff," he said, pointing to my place in formation at the end of his squad. My squad was the third of four columns with about eight kids each. Everyone was standing at parade rest. Some kids were bobbing back and forth on their heels and others were looking front like their necks were cemented. The ones who were looking front all had the red stripe on their hats. The others had a navy blue stripe. I assumed I was one of the new boy red stripers and looked front, staring at the back of this kid who had a bunch of veins in his neck branching all over the place like blue ivy.

Hillcrest stepped in front of me and kicked my feet further apart.

"Now this is pretty simple, Tegroff," he said. "When you take a shit, can you wipe your ass without falling in?"

"Yes, sir," I said.

"All you have to do is follow the guy in front of you. Do whatever he does. Watch his feet and stay in step. Can you do that, Tegroff?"

"Yes, sir."

Moments later, another bugle played and a couple of older kids who stood by flags in front of their companies started giving commands, one after the other. *"Alpha Company, A-ten-shun!, Bravo Company, A-ten-shun!, Band Company, A-ten-shun!, Charlie Company, A-ten-shun!, Delta Company, A-ten-shun!"* I snapped to attention. *"Echo Company, A-ten-shun!"* Following each command was this thunderous pounding noise from all of the companies clicking their heels on the guard path.

All of the sudden, in the middle of the lawn, six kids appeared, marching in single file, cutting the green moat in half. A bunch of silvery ornaments glinted off their shoulders like some kind of *Star Trek* costume jewelry. Everyone was completely quiet, except for all of the birds that were chirping in the trees.

The squad in the middle of the lawn stopped marching and this pale stocky kid peeled off, pivoted, and halted in front of the other five.

"Report!" he yelled.

"Alpha Company reports all present! Bravo

Company reports two men absent! Band Company reports all present! Charlie Company reports all present! Delta Company reports all present! Echo Company reports three men absent!"

After all of the company commanders had given their reports, they saluted the pale stocky kid, and he gave this completely overdramatic salute back to them, like his arm was made out of steel. After all of the saluting, the stocky kid did a twirl and saluted a kid who was in the middle of the command squad. Then the kid in the middle said, *"Company commanders, march your companies off to the dining hall!"* and he saluted and all of the kids standing by their flags saluted back.

A snare drum started rattling off a cadence and I could see the different companies maneuvering out of the corner of my eye.

"Right, *face!"* our company commander yelled at the top of his lungs. I tried to imitate everyone around me and pivoted to the right. "Forward, march!" Everyone started marching with their left foot, but I started with my right. I must have looked like a real genius, changing the step and trying to get in sync with everyone. A kid with a clipboard who was marching next to me yelled, "Dig it in, Delta!" and everyone started pounding their left heels into the ground. That helped me to keep the step. I could see all of the leaves twinkling in the morning sun as the guard path emptied on our way to the mess hall.

At breakfast, they announced the winner of the command reveille. Everyone held their breath. A lanky guy with gold diamonds on his shoulders, the important-looking one from the middle of the single squad, stepped up to this microphone podium. He looked very serious and unfolded this piece of paper like he was about to announce Best Picture at the Academy Awards. He pulled the microphone up to his mouth and cleared his throat. "The winner of this morning's command reveille is . . . Delta Company. They will eat first."

Everyone around me at the Delta Company tables cheered like a centerfold model had just exposed an upper thigh. The six guys at my table all high-fived each other. I actually saw Hillcrest smile for the first time. He had gray smoker's teeth. The sight of his teeth made me want to put off eating for a few minutes.

A kid knocked on our table and everyone got up and rushed to the front of the cafeteria, where the food line was.

A kid with curly red hair, who was at my table, told me to stand at attention in line. His nametag said *Warner*. He had two stripes on each shoulder.

"Make sure you ask for permission to be seated when you sit down," he whispered. "And ask to use the salt and pepper," he said out of the side of his mouth. "And don't start eating till he gives you *at ease*." I couldn't really tell what the kid looked like yet because I had to look toward the front.

When I reached the point where you grab your plate and silverware, Warner told me I could relax and get my food. He had freckles all over his face, like someone had splashed him with tomato paste.

"Thanks," I said, choosing the French toast and sausage platter.

"No problem. Believe me, I know the wrath of *The Hill*."

I laughed a little. "Is he always so serious?" I asked.

"You bet your ass. He broke me in last year. Three rules to remember: Never talk back, never say *but*, and never, *never ever*, make a comment about his weight. He made a kid quit school last semester. And he never touched him. Just scared the shit outta the poor bastard."

Hillcrest was loading some bread in the toast

rack. His fat was bulging out the sides of his pants. He looked like the Michelin Man.

I grabbed a cinnamon roll from the last station, and stood at attention in front of my seat.

"Sergeant Hillcrest, sir. New cadet Tegroff requests permission to be seated at the table, sir."

"Who taught you that?"

"No one, sir."

"Sit down. And keep your trap shut." I didn't start eating just yet. Hillcrest was watching me, waiting for me to reach for my fork. I just sat there at attention in my seat, looking front. In my peripheral vision I could see the shadow of Hillcrest's fat head jutting forward like a rhino's.

"At ease," he said through the soggy balls of toast in his mouth.

I really didn't feel like eating. My stomach was still in knots from everything. I looked down at my plate and felt something starting to come up. I swallowed a couple of times and tasted that battery acid that flies up your esophagus when you're about to puke.

I swallowed a few times and looked over at Warner, who was salting his eggs. I could tell he wanted to smile by the way he kept coughing into his napkin.

chapter eight

The Pain of Saluting

On my way to the shower, Warner stopped me in the hall and showed me how to parade around in the barracks. You have to do this system of walking called square corners, where you have to march on the right side of the hall like a robot. Whenever anyone with a stripe on his shoulder starts walking in the opposite direction, or even if he's just hanging out in the hallway, you have to stop and do a left face and pivot your body so it's square to the opposite wall. You can continue walking when the person is past you. If he just stands there, you have to say "Sir, excuse me, sir," and face him until he says "Post," which means you can go about your business.

Warner made me practice it in front of him a couple of times until I got the hang of it. I felt pretty stupid, pivoting around in my towel, with my soap and shampoo in my hand.

There were about six kids in the shower. Most of them were older, probably upperclassmen. I could tell they were older because they had hair on their chests and biceps the size of softballs.

The shower room was white and steamy. I walked up to a vacant nozzle, dropped my soap and shampoo, and cranked the water on. A muscular kid with a thick coat of soap all over his body snarled at me. He was the soapiest kid I'd ever seen in my life. I think he even had soap in his mouth and up his nose.

"That's an old boy shower," the kid said kind of loud, over the sizzling noise of the water. "New boys use those two on the end," he said, pointing to a couple of rusty shower heads that looked all washed up and sad. I grabbed my soap and shampoo and walked to the end of the shower room, still wrapped in my towel.

I cranked the water on and waited for it to get hot. I stood there, still wearing my towel, my palm in the spray of water, waiting for a rush of warmth. I must have looked like a complete moron with my towel on and all. I guess I'm not the type of person who likes to broadcast to the entire world that I'm what is known as a late bloomer. I'd rather wear my towel and look like a moron than expose my underdeveloped equipment to the rest of the hairy kids in Delta Company.

The water didn't feel like it would ever get warmer. In fact, it felt like it had gotten colder. I finally decided to shed my towel and stand underneath. You have to wash yourself. If you don't, you'll wind up smelling up elevators. The water was ice-cold. I never showered so fast in my life. I made these furious wrenching movements while I washed. I probably looked like a spastic drug fiend.

Some of the older guys were chuckling and pointing at me under their hot steamy water.

On my way to class I passed by that rock statue. Everyone saluted it like they were completely brainwashed, like if they didn't, it would turn into a monster and run them down with a chain saw or something.

This old fartbag in a green uniform stopped me and told me to stand at attention. His nametag read *Col. Perdue*. He was a zillion years old, really tall, and had these thick, black-framed, Jerry Lewis look-alike glasses on.

"Are you the new cadet, son?" he asked.

"Yes, sir," I said, staring at his Adam's apple.

"Has anyone taught you the tradition of the Beacon?"

"No, sir," I said, moving my feet slightly further apart, fearing they weren't forty-five degrees, that he'd slam down on them with his heel like Hillcrest.

"Well, I'll give you a quick lesson," he said, clearing his throat. "Every time you pass this monument, you salute it. It's a commemorative statue built in tribute to the school's *founder*. You know how to salute, cadet?"

"No, sir."

He took my right arm, bent it at the elbow, flattened my hand, made it stiff, and guided it to the tip of my right eyebrow.

"Just like that," he said. "You salute anyone with silver pips on his shoulder, anyone with a green uniform, and always, *always* salute the Beacon. It's a gesture of respect."

"Yes, sir," I said, shoving more rules into my brain.

"Carry on." Colonel Perdue walked away from me and saluted the Beacon with a completely proud look on his face. I turned toward the school buildings and went to class.

□ □ □

My algebra teacher, Mr. Flism, was one of the strangest old fartbags I'd ever seen in my life. First of all, what kind of name is Flism? I mean, there's only one *vowel* in it. If you say it fast enough, it sounds like you're drooling on yourself.

He was really tall and skinny and walked like he'd just crapped his pants while riding a horse, with his legs all bowed and out of sync with the rest of his body. His face was infected with wrinkles and looked like a dried-out apple. His eyes were little slits of dirty water, and his eyebrows were constantly pinched together. When he talked, he sounded like a tuba, with this really deep, blurting voice.

He was teaching us how to balance equations. This kid in the front row, who had a birthmark on the back of his neck shaped like the state of Maine, fell asleep flat on his face and started to snore. Mr. Flism took these two humongous steps toward him and grabbed a fistful of the kid's hair. The kid sprang out of his chair and turned completely red. Mr. Flism made him stand in the corner on one leg and balance a giant blackboard eraser on his head for the rest of the class.

Every so often, I'd glance over at him and watch his leg wobbling. What was really funny was that when Mr. Flism had to wipe something from the board, he just grabbed the giant eraser off the top of the kid's head. When he was finished, he'd walk back over and put it back on top, smacking the chalky side in the kid's hair.

After lunch, I picked up my books and a set of black nametags from the cadet store. The books were really heavy. On my way back to the barracks, I saw a kid with silver pips glinting on his shoulders walking toward me by the library. I knew I had to salute him, but it was almost impossible because both of my arms were totally filled with books. So I hid out behind this thorny bush next to the library entrance. I bent down kind of low and peered through the top of the bush, where the branches weren't quite as thick.

When he passed by I crouched as low as I could, and at the lowest point of my crouch I felt this sharp stab right between my butt cheeks. I tried to swallow my scream, but some of it burst out and I shook the bush with my arms because I had to clutch my can. The kid with the pips on his shoulders jumped in the air and got in this crazy defensive stance. My books fell all over me and flipped out in front of the library steps. The kid came over and looked over the bush. I was clutching my can and moaning.

"Cadet," he said, "what the hell are you doing? You scared the shit outta me."

I came out from behind the bush and stood at attention, gripping where it hurt with my fists which were supposed to be at my sides.

"Sir," I said, rubbing my ass. "I dropped one of my books coming out of the library and it landed behind that bush there, and when I bent down to pick it up, I sat on something sharp. I think I'm bleeding, sir."

"Turn around," he said. I felt like I was modeling for some kind of faggola G.I. Joe magazine or something, flouncing around and putting my can on display.

After a couple of seconds he came over and brushed some stuff off my back.

"You're OK," he said. "Next time watch where you're squatting. There are stakes all over the campus, where they plant things. Be careful."

"Yes, sir," I said, continuing to rub the sore spot on my ass. He helped me collect my books, and pulled one of my nametags out of the bush.

"Tegroff, huh?"

"Yes, sir."

"You must be new."

"Yes, sir."

"I'm Lieutenant Tomisac."

"Nice to meet you, sir," I said. He fixed the nametag on my sweater and brushed some more crap off my shoulder.

"Watch out for those stakes," he said, walking into the library.

"Yes, sir," I replied, trying to remember what hand I was supposed to salute with.

chapter nine
A Couple of Punches

When I reached Glenwood Hall, I square-cornered it to my room. There were a couple of brown suitcases in front of the sink, another foot-locker flush next to mine with a boom box resting on top of it, and a set of football pads on one of the desks. A faded poster of Malcolm X loomed over the desk.

Underneath the poster, a long, leather necklace dangled from this miniature, wooden tree. There was a red emblem the size of a hamburger patty with a quarter moon and a star in the middle. Also on the desk was a dark brown crucifix with Jesus on the cross, only this wasn't your everyday Sunday School Jesus. This was a *black* version of Jesus.

I dropped my books on my desk and stored my extra nametags in the footlocker. I walked over to the sink and looked at the suitcases. Just as I was about to bend down and read the tags attached to the handle, Hillcrest walked into the room. I stood at attention and stared at my acorny reflection in the medicine chest mirror.

"Well, Tegroff," Hillcrest said, "you are no longer the only new boy on campus with his own room. At ease. Say hi to your new roommate." On the word "roommate," a black kid walked into the room, carrying a leather clothing bag.

"Tegroff," Hillcrest said, "meet Truvoy Shockley. Shockley, meet Mr. Mike Tegroff. Or is it Jackoff? I hope you two lovebirds enjoy this arrangement," he said over his shoulder as he left.

Truvoy was about six feet tall and had shoulders as wide as a bookcase. He was wearing his class grays. His head was almost completely bald and looked like a light brown Milk Dud. He walked over to his desk and pulled his sweater off and started unbuttoning his blue shirt.

"When'd you get here?" he asked in a very deep voice as he hung the clothing bag in his closet.

"Yesterday," I said, watching his shoulder muscles bulge and ripple as he lifted his clothing bag and hooked it on the dowel. "Are you a new boy?" I asked.

"You got it. They'd never mix an old boy with a new boy. Those assholes have so many rules you'd think you're in prison."

"Tell me about it," I said. "I never thought I'd have to do the G.I. Joe shuffle just to walk down the hall." He smiled a little and shook his head. "When'd you get here?" I asked.

"Since football camp."

"How long's that been?"

"About a month. Two weeks before school."

"What position do you play?" I asked.

"Tailback."

He walked over to the desk, grabbed his shoulder pads, and placed them in his closet. Then he went into his footlocker and grabbed a bottle of lotion and squirted some on his hand. He pulled his pant cuffs up to his knees and started masaging the lotion into his calves. The room started to smell all sweet and cocoa buttery.

"Where you from?" he asked.

"Chicago," I said, stacking my books on my desk. "How 'bout you?"

"Detroit."

He was really going at it with the lotion.

"You a freshman?" he asked.

"Yeah," I said. "Are you?"

"Junior." He looked like he was twenty-three.

"Where was your room before?" I asked.

"They transferred me here from Echo Company," Truvoy said, squirting more lotion into his palm. "Other side of campus."

"Why?" I asked, noticing the lack of hair on his legs.

"Because I had what you might call a *disagreement* with First Sergeant Nealy."

"What happened?" I asked.

"He told me to drop and I punched him in the mouth."

"Why'd he drop you?"

"Because I got a *demerit* this morning. My back button fell off when I was putting my pants on. And no one in my squad had a sewing kit."

"So why didn't you drop?" I asked, feeling the soreness aching in my shoulders and chest from all of Hillcrest's push-ups.

"Because he called me a nigger." Truvoy looked at me directly in the eyes without blinking and stopped the bit with the lotion. "He said *drop, nigger, drop*. So I punched the jackass in his face. He don't know me from a can of *paint*!"

I started tapping my foot really fast.

"So what's gonna happen to you?" I asked.

"Guard path. Twenty hours."

"What happened to the first sergeant?"

"Nothing."

"Why not?"

"Nealy filled out the report. The jackass first sergeant *always* fills out the report."

Truvoy rubbed some more lotion into his face and changed into his coveralls. He started walking out of the room.

"Where you going?" I asked.

"Guard path. I have to get an hour in before practice."

"What about school?"

"I have gym. Offensive line coach runs the class." He did a right face and disappeared.

At dinner, Hillcrest introduced my new roommate to the rest of the table. Truvoy sat across from me, next to Warner. Whenever he wanted to sit down, he didn't ask for permission with very much enthusiasm. In fact, he had this distant look on his face and kind of mumbled his words. Hillcrest never gave him a problem, though, just said "At ease, Shockley," and let him sit down. Whenever I wanted to be seated, though, Fat Boy had to give me a headache. I didn't even get a chance to eat because every time I'd go to put a fork in my mouth, Hillcrest would ask me a question that would have absolutely nothing to do with anything.

One time, he said I was talking too fast. Another time, when I asked to use the salt, he said I wasn't looking front, even though I was. Hillcrest turned the simple pleasure of eating a meal into a complete pain in the ass. I started to dread going to the mess hall.

After dinner, I grabbed my ball and headed to the field house. I shot around at one of the side hoops all by myself. There were a lot of kids shooting at the main baskets with the break-away rims, but I like shooting at the side because you get more shots, and you can think about things without worrying about everyone else grabbing your ball.

My jumper was really clicking. I hit about ten in a row from eighteen feet. It felt good to do something besides reverse zero movements and square corners. It was refreshing to feel my leg muscles being worked again.

I did a couple of figure eight dribbles around my legs to get a feel for the ball, and then launched about fifteen more jumpers, mostly twenty-footers. A kid with thick arms who was about my height came over by me with his ball. He had dark brown hair, a couple of freckles on his nose, and braces. He took a couple of shots.

"We're gonna run some full court. Wanna play?" He didn't look at me when he talked, just concentrated on the basket.

"Yeah, sure," I said.

He stared down at my shoes.

"Where'dya get the Jordans?" he asked.

"My mom got 'em for me."

"New boy, huh?"

"I got here yesterday."

He did a couple of dribbles between his legs and fixed the ball under his armpit.

"You gonna try out for the team?"

"Sure."

"Does the coach know?"

"Yeah. I got him for English."

"What position do you play?" he asked.

"Point guard," I replied. "I can play a little off guard, too."

"Aren't you a little tall to be playing point guard?" he said. "You look more like a small forward to me."

I just shrugged my shoulders.

"I was the starting point guard on the JV last

year and I don't plan on giving up the spot."

He walked away, dribbling between his legs and behind his back.

To choose sides, we all shot from the top of the key. The first five were on one team and the second five made up the other. A couple of kids didn't make their shots and got all steamed and slammed the ball down.

I shot eighth and made mine so I was on the second team. The kid with the thick arms, dark brown hair, and braces was the first one to shoot and he made his.

"Play to eleven," he said, like he was the leader of the whole group. "Win by two."

I had a tall, skinny black kid on my team, who was a pretty good inside player. I could tell he'd gone to basketball camps by the way he posted up and called for the ball. He had a soft shooting touch and always blocked his man out when he rebounded. He made our first two baskets. After him, though, my team was pretty bad.

This kid who wore running shoes kept clapping his hands and screaming for the ball like he'd explode if he didn't touch it. One time, I passed him the ball on the baseline and he made this retarded move, twisting his body up like a palsy and traveling all over the place. When he shot the ball it slammed off the backboard and completely missed the rim.

Another kid with goggles was a decent offensive player, but he didn't know the first thing about defense. His man kept grabbing offensive rebounds and putting them back in.

The score was tied at eight and the kid with thick arms and braces was bringing up the ball. I was playing really good defense on him, making him turn a lot and switch over to his weaker, left hand. "Hufford," one of his teammates yelled, "I'm open." I had my hand in the passing lane and he tried to dump it in but I deflected the side of the ball. The lanky black kid on my team stole it, passed it to me, and filled the lane for a fast break. Hufford yelled *"Fuck,"* and sprinted back on defense with a frustrated look on his face. I shuffled a pass to the black kid, and he returned a really nifty pass to me, behind his back, just as Hufford was lunging for the steal. I scored the basket and tapped fists with my teammate while we ran back on defense.

The other team missed two shots and then we scored. The kid with goggles made a freethrow line banker, and the black kid hit a fadeaway jump shot to score the last basket. We'd won the game.

"What's your name?" the black kid asked, toweling himself off after the game.

"Mike," I said.

"You got a nice game. Some sweet passes."

"Thanks," I said.

"I'm Spoon. Spoon Benson. You made Hufford look pretty stupid out there. You're gonna challenge him for a spot."

"I just played hard." He offered his towel and I took it and wiped my arms.

"You a freshman?" I asked him, handing back the towel.

"Sophomore. I was reserve center on the JV last year. Will you be here tomorrow?" he asked, turning to leave.

"Sure," I said. "I'll be here."

Spoon walked out with his towel and everyone followed, except for Hufford, who was stretching out his calves next to the bleachers.

After I played, I cooled down, shooting some jump shots by myself. I started with some ten-footers at the side basket and gradually worked out to fifteen feet. Hufford came over with his ball.

"One-on-one?" he asked.

"Yeah. Sure," I said. "My ball or yours?"

"Mine," he said. He had one of those indoor-outdoor specials that you can't grip because it's half plastic. "Play to seven," he said. "Shoot for the ball." He took a shot at the top of the key and missed. It was my ball. "Make it take it," he said, handing me the ball.

I took two quick dribbles to my left and pulled up. Swish. I made the same move and scored again. Hufford came a little closer on defense and started bellying up to me, so I drove right around him with a quick step and made a left-handed lay-up. It was three to nothing. On my fourth possession, I missed a long jump shot and he grabbed the rebound. He dribbled between his legs a couple of times and made a double-pump shot, banking it off the glass. Then he faked this really good crossover and went in for a lay-up, slapping the glass. He was pretty quick, and he could jump as high as me, so I gave him a defensive cushion like Coach Forrestall had taught me. He pulled up in my face and hit a fifteen-foot jump shot. It was three to three.

On his next possession, he tried to pull up in my face again, but I slapped the ball away and grabbed it. He bellied up to me again. I exploded past him and scored another lay-up. Then I hit a fadeaway jump shot. The score was five to three, in my favor. I tried to cross over in front of him like Tim Hardaway of the Golden State Warriors does, but he stole the ball and scored another lay-up.

He missed two more shots, and I scored twice, one on a fadeaway jumper, and one on a complete dipsy-doo luck shot that I flicked under his arm. It rattled around the rim, kissed the glass, and died through the twine of the net. I'd won the game.

He slammed the ball down, and got up in my face. His cheeks were all flushed, flaring like little red islands. I started to back off because he was all sweaty and he smelled like athlete's foot. He pushed me in the chest kind of hard. My stomach dropped. He came up close and pushed me again, this time right in the Adam's apple, but I just stood there, frozen. Then he cocked back and drove a punch in my ear. I felt my knees give out and I hit the floor. I grabbed at the pain with both hands. Hufford crouched over me with his fists clenched, waiting for me to get up. His arms were bulging pretty thick, with a couple of veins spidering down his forearms.

I didn't want to get up, since I thought maybe he'd leave me alone if I stayed down. I just clamped my eyes shut and tucked my head into my chest. All I could hear were the halogen lights buzzing. I just closed my eyes and held my ear.

Eventually, he walked away. I think I heard him call me a pussy before he left. The front doors crashed shut, echoing in the empty gym. I just lay there with my knees in my chest, holding my ear at center court.

The sky had fallen from a deep, purplish-blue into a balmy orange. The air chilled the sweat into my skin. I was all clammy and sorry, carrying my ball under my left arm and pressing against my bloody ear. I felt like disappearing under some loose change.

Off on the guard path, in the graying distance of the twilight, the kid from the day before was marching alone with his rifle. He made the same movements again, resting the rifle on his right shoulder, pacing twenty yards, working it like a lever, flipping it off his shoulder to land by his right foot, and then pivoting completely around, returning the rifle to his shoulder to march in the opposite direction. He repeated everything over and over again, like one of those sorry-looking, silent, black-and-white super-eight flicks you watch through a movie box at the carnival.

I watched him while I leaned up against the

Beacon, pressing my ear. I stood there for a couple of minutes. I grabbed part of a broken tree branch off the ground and started writing things in the dirt by the flowers while I watched him.

For some reason, his ghost-like figure made me feel a little better. Maybe it was because I felt so terrible, and watching him made me feel like I wasn't the only one, like there was someone else out there who wasn't having such a great time.

I looked down to see what I'd written in the dirt. It said:

Dear Mom and Alice,
HELP.

chapter ten

Cocoa Butter

I lifted up the lid of my footlocker and grabbed my box of cotton balls. Truvoy was tilting back in his chair, reading a book. I went to the medicine chest mirror and dabbed the blood from my ear with the cotton ball.

"What happened?" Truvoy asked.

"Um," I said, "I got elbowed going for a rebound."

"You're bleeding," he said.

"Yeah, I know," I said. "It's not too serious."

"You better get some alcohol on that."

"It looks OK," I said, feeling the sting of the cotton.

"Here," Truvoy said, lunging for his footlocker, grabbing a bottle of rubbing alcohol.

He shook the bottle with a cotton ball over the

opening and dabbed at my ear. It felt like a hornet's nest had been let loose on the side of my head. I jumped a little and flung my arm out from the stinging, but everything kind of went numb after a couple of seconds.

"Whoever clocked you has pretty sharp elbows," Truvoy said, fixing me up. He smelled like cocoa butter. "You're lucky that joker missed your eye." He cleaned it a couple more times and threw the bloody cotton balls in the wastebasket.

"Thanks," I said.

Truvoy walked back over to his desk and started reading again. I grabbed my algebra book and sat down. I balanced a couple of equations for a few minutes and then got really bored. If there's one thing I can't stand it's math. I'll bet the guy who invented math was one of those lonely geniuses who reads porno magazines and plays with himself a lot.

I closed my book and decided to write Mom and Alice a letter. I knew that I couldn't mail it because I didn't have their address, but for some reason I felt like I had to get something down on paper. I grabbed a pen and a notebook from my footlocker and started to write. It went like this:

Dear Mom and Alice,

Just thought I'd write to say hi. As you probably know by now, I'm at this school where everyone thinks they're G.I. Joe. My squad leader's a whale. He weighs about two hundred fifty pounds and looks like the Michelin Man. He makes me do a lot of push-ups. Next time you see me I'll probably be all muscular and I'll have to get new clothes. My roommate is pretty cool. His name is Truvoy Shockley. He's on the football team and he's cut with muscles. He's from Detroit.

I played basketball today and beat this hotshot in a game of one-on-one. My jumper is really on. You should see my hair. I look like Colonel Sanders' illegitimate son. My head is shaped like an acorn.

If you think of it, maybe you could come out for a visit? Maybe the play will come to Milwaukee? ~~God I miss you guys. I cried yesterday.~~

Cosette, how's the show? Have you started a fan club yet? Don't forget to send me an autographed picture.

Love,
Mike

I folded the letter up, slid it into an envelope, and stored it in my top drawer.

Truvoy walked over to his footlocker and grabbed his lotion again. He squirted a mound in his hand, pulled his pant leg up, and started massaging his calves again.

"How come you use so much lotion?" I asked.

"My skin dries out a lot from football. From the salt in my sweat. If I don't moisturize, I get scaly. Like a fish." I looked over at the book on his desk. It was *The Autobiography of Malcolm X.*

"Did you see the movie?" Truvoy asked me.

"Um . . . no. I'm gonna check it out on video, though."

All of a sudden, Hillcrest walked in the room. Truvoy and I froze at attention.

"What the hell are you doing out of your seat, Jackoff?" Then he turned to Truvoy and said, "At ease, Shockley." Truvoy put his lotion away and stuck a Q-Tip in his ear. I stayed at attention, staring at Fat Boy's gruesome teeth. "What the hell are you doing out of your seat, Tegroff?"

"I was just looking at my roommate's book, sir," I said.

"*I was just looking at my roommate's book, sir,*" he said, mocking me with a feminine sneer in his voice. "You never, *never ever,* leave your seat during study hours. Do you understand that, Jackoff?"

"Yes, sir," I replied.

"Good," he said. "Now drop and give me twenty so you don't forget."

I dropped and started pumping them off. At fifteen, my arms started trembling and I didn't think I was going to make it. It was hard to count out loud, and I couldn't say anything after seventeen because I was out of breath.

"What?" Hillcrest said. "I can't hear you counting, Tegroff. You better start over."

"I don't know if I can—"

"Do it!"

"Yes, sir." I took a couple of deep breaths and started over. I had to go really slow, and my arms were wobbling. I must have looked like a complete sissy in front of Truvoy, unable to do a couple of lousy push-ups. When I was finished and painfully out of breath, Hillcrest ordered me to stay in position for about a minute. He laughed a little bit while my arms were spazzing out.

"You're such a goddamn pussy, Tegroff," he said, chuckling and completely cracking himself up. "Get up."

I stood at attention. Some sweat had rolled down the side of my head and my ear was stinging again.

"Get in your fucking seat and stay there, Jackoff,"

he said, leaving the room with all of his blubber.

"He doesn't like you much, does he?" Truvoy said while I stared blankly at my algebra book.

"No. Guess not. I never did *anything* to the fat bastard."

"He's just tryin' to fuck with you. To mess with your head. It's all about intimidation here. Jokers like him thrive on that shit."

"I've only been here a couple of days and he's been riding me the whole time," I said.

"That's how it was for me in Echo. Nealy wouldn't let up at all. That joker kept diggin' in my mind with his goddamn head games. Last Thursday, after taps, he made me scrub all of the urinals with my toothbrush. Because I wouldn't cut my hair low. Because I wouldn't wear my hair like the rest of these blind punks. I stayed up till two-thirty. The next day, that joker marched me to the barber and told Godzilla to shave it off. Bald. Like an eight ball. I couldn't take it anymore. He was treatin' me like a *slave*. A *slave*. No one treats Truvoy Shockley like a slave. And no *white boy* will ever get away with calling me nigger. I don't care how many jacked-up stripes he has on his shoulder. I don't care. There comes a point when you have to take a stand."

My ear started bleeding again. I stood up, and slowly walked over to my footlocker. I flipped the lid and grabbed another cotton ball. I made my way over to the medicine chest, kind of hoping, but not really hoping, that Hillcrest would walk in again.

That night, after taps had blown, someone flashed his hand in our doorway and flicked the light off. Truvoy turned a few times in the top bed, making the whole bunk squeak. It was really dark in the room, except for a knife of light that bent in from the hallway.

"So tell me something, Mike," Truvoy said in a soft, deep voice. "How'd you wind up here?" It was nice to hear someone call me Mike for a change.

"I don't know really," I said. "It all happened so fast. I guess I was kind of dumped here."

"*Dumped* here?"

"I'll make a long story short," I said. "My little sister's an actress and she's in this play that tours all around the country. I was supposed to stay with my dad, but his wife didn't want me around. So I'm here."

"So your little sister gets famous and you get this," he said. I didn't say anything, just turned in my bunk. "And your pop's new batch of booty sends you away."

"I guess you could say that."

"That's pretty rough."

He turned in his bed.

"So, your parents ain't together?" he asked.

"They split up a while ago."

"How old were you?"

"Five."

"Why'd they split up?" he asked. I thought about that for a second.

"I don't know. I never asked." I looked out the window. The parking lot was almost empty, except for a school van and an old station wagon.

"Are your p's together?" I asked.

"No," he said. "My pops died when I was pretty young."

"Sorry."

"Yeah. So am I," he said.

I didn't say anything for a few minutes. I heard the church bell gong and looked out at the moon-light. The bunk squeaked a few more times.

"Truvoy, how'd *you* wind up here?" I asked.

"Oh, I did somethin' pretty stupid."

"What?"

"I robbed a money machine."

"You did?"

"Yup."

"How?"

"My boy Hollis and me stuck up the cat who changes the machine. His partner musta been out buying doughnuts or something. We didn't even use a real gun."

"You didn't?" I asked.

"Nope. Man we used a *starter's pistol*. Hollis bought it off the track coach. Looked like a twenty-two, though," Truvoy said, kind of laughing.

"Wow."

After a minute, Truvoy stopped laughing.

"So the courts sent you?" I asked, remembering Dad telling me that St. Matthew's Military Academy was a school full of *good kids*, the *cream of the crop*.

"No. The jackasses never caught me."

"So what happened?" I asked.

"My moms found the stash."

"How much'dya steal?"

"Twelve gees."

"*Twelve thousand dollars?* Jeezus Christmas, Truvoy! What were you planning to do with the money?"

"I was going to go down south with Hollis. He had a brother in New Orleans."

"Your mom turn you in?"

"No."

"What happened?" I asked.

"She made me use it to pay for this place. Her and *Roger* thought the discipline would do me good."

"Who's Roger?" I asked, turning on my side for a more comfortable position.

"Her *white* boyfriend."

After that we were silent. Outside I could hear the faint noise of cars cutting through wind, making their way on a distant highway.

chapter eleven

Looking for a Tree to Climb

"**D**efine yourself as a leader. I want *your* definition of leadership. You might have to look inside yourself to find it. That's your assignment for Friday," Captain Peck said at the end of Military Training I. "Leadership is the process in which you influence others to accomplish the mission. I don't want that paraphrased. I want *your* conception of leadership. Stay out of the dictionary. Look in the mirror."

Captain Peck was this really intense Vietnam vet who walked with a limp. He had a tough-looking goatee, and sucked on a wooden match.

During class, he lectured about the process of leadership and how you have to learn how to be a *follower* before you can take on the role of a leader.

I pictured Hillcrest following Charles Manson.

He also told this really gruesome story about how he'd lost his right testicle in the war. It got severed by some flying shrapnel. He said a guy in his own platoon had thrown the grenade, not knowing that Captain Peck was in this straw hut where he was evacuating a small baby. The baby's hands had been blown off. Captain Peck said the baby was crying like mad, and then there was a loud noise and he felt something rip and burn. He said the pain of burning shrapnel doesn't go away like a sore throat. He said it smolders for a very long time.

He said the baby didn't make it, that it died in his arms. He didn't blink when he said that.

In algebra, the same kid with the birthmark on his neck dozed off again. Mr. Flism threw a box of chalk at him. The kid woke up flailing his arms. This time, Mr. Flism made him stand on top of his desk and sing the national anthem. The kid didn't think Mr. Flism was serious, and then he was given a choice of either performing for the class or walking ten hours of guard path. So he reluctantly climbed on top of his desk, nervously looked all around the room, and cleared his throat. When Mr. Flism wasn't watching, this bozo with one eyebrow flipped the bird to the kid who'd fallen asleep. The kid messed up at the part when you're supposed to sing *and the rocket's red glare* and sang *and the rocket's red hair* instead. Everyone laughed like crazy. He had a really bad voice. It cracked three or four times.

In most of my other classes I kept looking at everyone's shoes and wondering how long it took to shine them.

In English we had to read a short story called "The Golden Tree," about a kid whose parents had died. He was adopted by a lonely old lady who played bridge a lot and taught him how to slow dance and bake cookies. Every afternoon, the kid would climb this huge oak tree in the backyard, where he'd feel really sorry for himself and eat leaves and think about his parents. On his birthday, he climbed really high, all the way to the top, and jumped off into the sunset.

As a reader you were supposed to think he flew away like a bird and became free, like he discovered some kind of flouncy happiness, but I thought the poor kid committed suicide and was completely sad.

After we read it, we were supposed to write a paragraph on our response to the story. I wrote that I thought the kid was a loser, and instead of feeling sorry for himself in that tree all the time, he should have made the best of the situation and learned to like slow dancing with the old woman. I also mentioned that I thought the writing style was a little half-baked, that the author probably wrote it so he could make himself bawl.

I handed in my paper and returned to my seat. While I sorted out all of my notebooks and folders, Mr. Savery put his hand on my shoulder.

"How's it going?" he asked, crossing his arms in front of his chest. His Elvis hairdo looked like a plastic helmet.

"Pretty good," I said. "I'm adjusting."

"Spoon Benson tells me you have a nice floor game. We're looking for a good floor leader."

"Spoon's a good inside player," I said. "He can fill the lane on the break, too."

"He said you're a heckuva passer," Mr. Savery said, smiling.

"Didn't Hufford start at point last year?" I asked, rubbing my ear, remembering how much it rang after he'd punched me.

"Last year was last year. I'm new just like you. Everyone has a fair shot in my book. I just want to put the best combination on the floor. It's as simple as that." I nodded my head agreeably and fixed my books under my arm.

"We'll be having a meeting pretty soon," he said. "To get tryouts organized and shoe sizes and stuff like that. I'll let you know." He picked up my pen that I had dropped next to his feet. "Remember, Mike. I'm here if you need anything. Anything at all. Just knock on my door."

"I will," I said, looking out the window for a tree to climb. "Thanks, Mr. Savery."

On my way back to the barracks, I could hear the sounds of shoulder pads popping in the distance. Every thirty seconds or so a whistle would blow, and then came the deep, fiberglass-against-fiberglass detonation. I crossed the guard path and, off in a distant field, I could see the football team doing hitting drills. Their canvas practice jerseys were full of grass stains. Cleat marks were all over the grass, and patches of dried mud infected the drill area. One of the portable goal posts was crooked. A kid with no pads on was kicking field goals through the supports.

When I got closer I could make out the names on the back of the jerseys.

A huge iron blocking plow that looked like a farming relic from the Civil War days was planted in the middle of the field, at the fifty-yard line. It was rusted all over the place and looked like it weighed a ton.

A big fat guy with a bag of chew in his hand was standing next to the blocking plow. He was the one blowing the whistle. There was a huge line in back of one of the other coaches. Every time the fat coach would blow his whistle the kid at the front of the line would hustle a few steps forward and get in a three-point stance. At the sound of the second whistle, he would burst forward and heave his shoulder into the blocking plow. After it was driven forward ten yards, the coach would blow his whistle again, signaling him to stop. Then the kid had to push the plow back to its original spot and run to the back of the line.

Truvoy was number thirty and had SHOCKLEY on the back of his jersey. In his helmet, he looked like some kind of futuristic bounty hunter. When he got to the front of the line, I moved even closer and hid behind an old oak tree. The coach holding the bag of chew blew his whistle. Truvoy sprinted forward a few yards and stopped. In his three-point stance he was angular and statuesque. On the second whistle, Truvoy sprang forward and drove his shoulder into the plow. It made a sound similar to the hood of a big Chevy slamming shut.

Truvoy drove his legs into the earth with fierce, chopping strides. After ten yards the coach blew the whistle again but Truvoy didn't stop. He didn't stop after twenty or thirty yards either. He kept pushing the blocking plow all the way through the end zone and nearly knocked over the portable goal post. The kid kicking field goals almost got slaughtered and had to jump out of the way.

There was a huge fence at the back of the end zone, about twelve feet high. All of the coaches started running toward Truvoy, who had taken his helmet off by now and was staring at the top of the fence. *"Shockley!"* they screamed. *"Shockley!"* Truvoy turned around and saw them heading toward him. For a second, I thought he was going to climb the fence, but by the time the fat coach had reached the end zone, Truvoy had already put his helmet back on. The coach slapped him on the top of the helmet and said something kind of loud but I couldn't quite make it out. Then Truvoy was on the ground, pumping off push-ups, one sir, two sir, three sir, all the way to thirty. When he finished, he got up and pushed the plow all the way back to the fifty-yard line, just as fast as he had pushed it into the end zone.

I never saw someone so strong in my life.

Later that evening, while climbing up the last couple of stairs before dinner, I could hear some really funky rap music resounding from my floor. As I square-cornered it to my room, Warner was leaning up against the shower door. I faced him and said "Sir, excuse me, sir." He told me to post and flashed a really nice smile at me.

The music was coming from my room. As I was about to enter, I saw Truvoy washing his face at the sink and doing this really cool dance step, shuffling his feet and vibrating his can like he was giving it to an imaginary girl. I stood there, laughing in the doorway, watching him. He could really move.

"What's up, Mike?" he said, rubbing soap into his face, still dancing, not the least bit embarrassed. I'll tell you, if someone walked in on me when I was flouncing around and vibrating my butt cheeks, I'd feel pretty embarrassed.

"Nothing," I said. "What are you doing? You look like you're laying the invisible man."

"The invisible *female*," he said, rinsing his face. "Vanessa Williams."

"Oh," I said. "I didn't know she made special appearances to new boys' rooms."

"Only ours."

Truvoy dried his face with a towel and turned the music down. He seemed to be in a pretty good mood. "Do you dance, Mike?" he asked.

"Yeah," I said. "Sure."

The only time I'd ever danced with a girl was at a sock hop after we'd beaten Laraway in the conference tournament. A girl named Cindy asked me to slow dance. She had long brown hair and a beauty mark above her lip. She told me that I smelled like a Howard Johnson's. I thought she was pretty sexy too, but I had to stay about a foot away from her body because I started swelling up.

After the dance, Cindy kissed me on the mouth and asked me if we could *go together*. I kind of froze up and told her I couldn't go anywhere because I had some homework to do, and left.

"Let's see what you can do," Truvoy said.

"Now?" I asked.

"Yeah, *now*," he said. "Put your money where your mouth is."

"Well," I said, my tongue tripping all over itself, "I kinda just like to slow dance mostly."

"You can't *fast dance?*"

"No. Not really," I said, wringing my hands together. "I feel pretty goofy."

"You *gotta* fast dance, Mike," Truvoy said. "How do you expect to get any booty?" I just smiled and started turning red. "You get booty, don't you?" I didn't say anything, just kept feeling my hands really hard. "You don't?" He laughed a couple of times. I felt like the reincarnation of Beaver Cleaver. "You haven't got your back out yet?!" he laughed. "OK, so you're a virgin," he said. "So what. You gotta start somewhere, right?"

"I don't know. I don't think I—"

"C'mon. I'll teach you." He raised the volume and started moving his can and flailing his arms around to the beat. "Feel the rhythm," he said, smiling, his knees smoothly bending with the bass. I just stood there with my feet cemented, watching his calves furrowing under his towel. "C'mon, Mike. You wanna get some booty someday, don't you? Try this," he said, bowing his legs and vibrating his butt cheeks. "It's called the German Smurf."

"The *what?*"

"The German Smurf, my man. You never heard of the *German Smurf?*"

"No."

"Booty's *guaranteed* if you know the German Smurf," he said, dancing effortlessly, his whole body bending and dipping to the rhythm. "What kind of joker goes through life without gettin' his back out?"

I tried to move a little, but felt really awkward.

"That's it," Truvoy said. "There you go. Move with the music. Blend with Vanessa." I pictured Vanessa Williams in front of me and tried to get kind of close to her, dropping my butt real low and kind of swiveling around. My lower back loosened up and I think I started to get the hang of it.

I know this sounds completely faggola, with me getting low and swiveling my can, but it was kind of fun, actually.

"That's it. *Yeah, boy*. Get Vanessa. Get that booty," Truvoy said as we both danced.

After a minute, Truvoy said, "Hold up. I want Vanessa back. She's black. We gotta get you a *white* girl."

"Bridget Fonda," I said, continuing to swivel my hips.

"Yeah," Truvoy said. "Bridget Fonda. Now there's a *fine* white girl. She's a little light in the ass, but she's fine." We both laughed and danced with our imaginary girls, flouncing all around the room to the music like a couple of faggolas.

"Yeah, Mike," Truvoy said. "Get that booty. Knock those boots like a *brother!*"

I think I actually started to look halfway decent because I felt like I was moving with the music, like the rhythm had actually gotten into my joints. Like I was actually *blending* with Bridget Fonda. Truvoy went over to the sink and started humping it. I just laughed and kept my distance from Bridget. I wasn't ready to get my back out yet.

I hadn't felt so good since I left home.

chapter thirteen

Agape

I couldn't play basketball after dinner because we had to go to compulsory chapel. Everyone filed into the walnut pews and fiddled with the missalettes. We were up pretty close, about three rows from the altar.

The inside of the chapel looked like some kind of medieval shrine, with racks of scented candles flickering in the mouths of stone alcoves.

The dimming outside light shone through the stained glass windows, casting oblong shadows off the jagged rocks, filling the walls with ghosts. The altar was made of marble. A huge, wood-carved, lacquer crucifix loomed over the offertory table. Jesus looked like he was in complete agony, with his thorny forehead wrinkled and his eyes wedged shut.

To the right of the table sat a tremendous, brass

pipe organ. An old Italian woman with a beehive hairdo and a mustache loomed over the keys and played a really depressing version of "Amazing Grace."

Truvoy sat to the right of me, and Warner leaned back on my left. Hillcrest was melting at the end of our pew like a big blob of grease. He looked like one of those giant Buddha dolls, with the fat in his neck folding over in heavy creases.

The chaplain had a swollen, sweaty face that looked like it had been sculpted from a canned ham. He directed everyone to turn to some page for the opening hymn. I grabbed a hymnal from the rack and leafed through to the song. It was called "Five Hundred Miles." I kind of lipped the words and looked around me. Warner was singing in this high-pitched, Judy Garland falsetto, and all of the kids next to him were singing too. Truvoy didn't even have a book in his hand, and just stared off into space.

After the song, a kid with a bunch of stripes on his shoulder stepped up to the podium and read a poem, entitled "Agape," about brotherly love. His lip was split open and swollen. His nametag said *Nealy*. It was the first sergeant who'd called my roommate a nigger. I glanced over at Truvoy again.

His face was so still it looked like it had been carved out of the side of a tree.

Then the chaplain read a couple of passages of scripture from the Bible about Abraham and his son, how God asked Abraham to kill his son, and how Abraham was going to do it because he was so completely in love with God, and then at the last minute, God told him he didn't have to go through with it, like he was just bluffing. It was a pretty half-baked story.

After the sermon, we had to chant the "Our Father," then we sang a closing hymn. I think it must have been the school fight song, because everyone stood up really fast and sang with enthusiasm, like Miss October was about to storm the altar. Part of the first verse went like this:

Onward Christian Soldiers
Marching as to war
With the cross of Jesus
Going on before . . .

Halfway through the song, this kid with fuzzy hair who sat in the pew in front of us turned around and made this face at Warner, flipping his eyelids up so they stuck and the pink showed.

Warner spazzed out. He tried to swallow his laughter, but a green booger shot out of his nose and landed on his cheek, next to his ear. It was totally disgusting. It looked like a little version of the Incredible Hulk clinging to his face, mixing in with all of his freckles. I laughed uncontrollably for a few seconds and then stopped, but my body kept spastically bobbing up and down because I was still cracking up inside.

I looked over and saw Hillcrest burning a stare right through me. My face got all hot and I stopped laughing. I stared down at my hymnal and tried to sing the last verse, but I couldn't find my place.

Back in the room, Truvoy slammed open his closet door and slipped into some coveralls. He looked really steamed, with this vein pulsing by his temple. He walked over to his footlocker and flipped up the lid kind of hard.

"What's wrong?" I asked, getting my books together before study hours.

"Did you see that joker up there? Did you see him?"

"Who?" I asked.

"*Nealy*. Did you see him reciting his little *love poem* real pretty? Poppin' off about *mutual respect* and *brotherly love*, and the rest of that bullshit. That white motherfucker doesn't know the first thing about it," he said, his eyebrows furrowing. "*Respect*. Phony motherfucker."

"Yeah," I said. "He seemed like kind of a jerk. Looked like you clocked him pretty good." Truvoy sat down at his desk and opened his Malcolm X book.

I pulled out a sheet of paper and started to write Mom and Alice again, but first, I wanted to get a drink of water and check out my ear in the mirror. Just as I was about to grab a cup from my foot-locker, Hillcrest walked in. Truvoy sprang to attention by his desk and I dropped my cup and stood stiff as a statue.

"Shockley," he said, "go stand by your closet and face the wall."

Truvoy said "Yes, sir," and walked over to his closet door, faced it, and stood at attention.

"So, Mr. Tegroff," Hillcrest said, "maybe you can fill me in on whatever was so goddamn *amusing* at chapel tonight. Maybe my brain was out to lunch 'cause it seems that I missed the joke." I didn't say anything, just stared at the medicine chest and felt my stomach slowly start to drop. "Well," he said, his hog face swelling, "I'm waiting, and you better come up with something *real* good because if your excuse doesn't light my fire, I'm gonna call my friend Little Jack Crappypants and I've heard he's been looking for something hot to dance around in, and you know what that means, right, Tegroff?"

"Yes, sir."

"Well, *speak!*"

"Sir," I said, "I don't know why I—"

"*Bullshit!* You have about zero seconds to start talking."

"But, sir," I said, "I really don't know why I—"

Then I felt his huge, fat hand smothering my Adam's apple. He picked me up by my neck and slammed me up against the wall. His eyes were wild, and his bagel face was bulging with pressure, and I felt my neck getting really thick and I couldn't talk because he was pressing so hard. My face was filling with blood and I couldn't breathe.

"*Why, Jackoff, why?*" he screamed, slamming me against the wall. I tried to say something, anything, but nothing would come out. My head started to get really heavy and I couldn't get my breath going. I felt the back of my head thumping into the wall, and my hands went up to his and I tried to pry them from my neck.

Then I saw two thick black arms wrap around Hillcrest's neck and he let go of me. I fell to the floor gasping for air. Truvoy had him in a headlock in the middle of the room. He had torn his coveralls and his arms were bulging out like brown, veiny softballs. He crouched over Hillcrest and squeezed his head. Hillcrest's face started to fill with a purplish color. He writhed his fat arms around as if to grab on to something but there was nothing to grab.

After a minute, Truvoy released him. Hillcrest gasped for air on the ground and coughed like he was choking on a hunk of steak. Truvoy stood over him. His chest heaved.

"Leave him alone," he said. "He ain't done nothin' to you." Truvoy was breathing fast and looked kind of scared. "He ain't done nothin'." He didn't blink. His eyes were dark as caves.

Hillcrest slowly hoisted himself up, grabbing at his fat neck and said, "Shockley, you just bought yourself a *ho lot a tru ble*." He kind of struggled to get the words out. His breath wouldn't come. "I know . . . a first ser . . . geant . . . who will *love* . . . to hear a . . . bout this."

Hillcrest got his balance, slowly turned, pushing off the wall, opened the door, and floundered out.

After a while, I walked back over to my desk and looked at the blank letter. My neck was throbbing and it hurt to swallow. I picked up my pen and sat there kind of stiff.

A few minutes passed. Eventually, I released my pen and crumpled up the piece of paper. I'd forgotten who I was going to write to.

chapter fourteen

The Dread of School Buses

The next morning, at first mess, the important kid with diamonds flashing on his shoulders stepped up to the podium, holding a manila file. "In light of next Saturday's football game against Wegman, and the conference cross-country meet on the golf course, the Commandant has issued a declaration of Parents' Weekend."

The whole mess hall cheered and tapped on their glasses with silverware. When the clinking became too loud, the kid at the microphone said, "At ease," and everything hushed.

"All new boys will have temporary visitation privileges, from Friday after classes through Sunday, immediately following third mess. *However*, new boys will *not* be able to leave the campus. The

Commandant has also issued a battalion police call for the grounds, which will be conducted this afternoon, following classes. Carry on."

While we ate, Truvoy stared down at his plate. When he asked to use the salt and pepper, he didn't even look up, he just mumbled the request for permission line and continued to stare at his eggs.

Hillcrest didn't eat much. Usually, he'd put away about three plates of pancakes and a couple of Bismarcks. The whole table was silent, like someone had died. Even Warner had a certain quiet about him.

When I ate, it still hurt to swallow. I couldn't seem to rub the feeling of Hillcrest's fat hand out of my neck.

Morning classes were a blur. They all seemed to be strung together like one long lecture. I floated from class to class like a ghost, seemingly right through the walls.

After lunch, Truvoy slipped on his coveralls, which he pinned at the shoulders where they'd torn, and headed to guard path. On his way out, he told me that I'd received a letter and pointed to my desk, where a white envelope rested. It was from Mom. I grabbed a pen from my top drawer and tore it open. It read:

Dear Michael,

Hi, honey. How are you? Dad told me about your
new school. He said you seemed real favorable about
it. I hope you like it. From what Dad said, it sounds
like a really neat place. He said the campus was
beautiful and that it had its own golf course. It's a
wonderful thing that Dad and Rayne have done for
us. I hope you appreciate all their help.

Philadelphia is a big city and not very far from
New York. It's kind of dirty, with a lot of taxicabs.
Alice and I feed the pigeons on the way to the
theater in this big park, where a lot of homeless
people always ask us for change. Alice gave a quarter
to an old man who called himself Flapjack Joe. He
was wearing a plastic bag and a headdress of leaves
in his hair. It's sad to see what happens to these
homeless people. I guess your mind starts to go when
you have no family or friends to be with.

Alice and I went to dinner last night with Grover,
her new agent. He took us to a lovely Indian restaurant
where the waitresses wear turbans. The food was hot
and spicy. Alice was a real hit. She asked our waitress
for a bottle of champagne and stuck a grain of brown
rice on her forehead so that she'd be in an "Indian"
mood. That really made Grover laugh. You know how
Alice can be a riot when she wants.

143

Grover is a very handsome man. He has kind eyes. He told me I had "commercial" hands, that I could do laundry detergent commercials and pose for jewelry store ads. He says that if Alice stays with the show many bigger roles will come her way, possibly TV!

Alice has been losing her voice a bit, but she uses Chloraseptic spray, which helps a lot. Last night her understudy had to perform for her. Her dressing room has a speaker from which you can hear the whole show. Her personal dresser calls her "Ms. Tegroff," and she's received several bouquets of flowers. I arranged them all over the hotel. It smells like a spring meadow.

Please write and tell us about your new school. Are you making a lot of new friends? Do they have a good basketball team? How are the shoes working out? Do you like your classes?

Alice wanted me to enclose her new headshot. I think she looks too old in it. I don't like her wearing so much makeup. The director's son asked her to go to a water slide with him next weekend. We have to get her a suit.

I miss you very much and wish we could all be together. I'm glad things have worked out for you. Just remember that it's for us. Write soon. Alice looks forward to hearing from you.

Love, Mom

□ □ □

I pulled out the picture of Alice. She did look older. She was wearing shadow on her lids, which made her eyes look huge and cartoony. And her hair was flowing all over her neck like she was starring in a soap opera. Her smile was forced, with an unnatural tug at the sides of her mouth. Down by the base of her neck she signed her name. It said:

To my favorite brother, Michael Jeffrey Tegroff.
Love, Alice (Little Cosette)

I rubbed the creases out and stuck it to the wall above my desk with some tape. I remembered what Truvoy had said the first night we became roommates. *So your little sister gets famous and you get this.* For a split second, I thought I was going to tear the picture off the wall and throw it in the trash, but I didn't. Instead, I grabbed the letter I had written to Mom and Alice out of my top drawer, pulled an envelope from my footlocker, stuffed it, wrote the address on the front, and placed it on top of my desk.

I pictured Mom and Alice at that Indian restaurant, where the waitresses wear turbans and dot their foreheads and snake music sneers through a light film of exotic, blue smoke. I envisioned Grover as a watered-down version of MacGuyver. I didn't like the way Mom called him handsome and talked about his eyes. I thought things were getting pretty solid between Mom and Charlie Brown. I know the guy isn't the second coming of Johnny Hollywood, but at least he seemed real interested in her, and he's musical, and he likes to play one-on-one with me, even though he isn't very good. What the hell kind of name is Grover anyway?

I tried to push these thoughts from my mind. I looked over at Truvoy's desk and saw his book resting in the middle of it. I picked it up, randomly opened to a page, and started reading. It said:

> In the summertime, at night, in addition to all the other things we did, some of us boys would slip out down the road, or across the pastures, and go "cooning" watermelons. White people always associated watermelons with Negroes, and they sometimes called Negroes "coons" among all the other names, and so stealing watermelons became "cooning" them. If white boys were doing it, it implied that they were only acting like Negroes. Whites have always hid-

den or justified all of the guilts they could
by ridiculing or blaming Negroes.

I thought about Truvoy and how he placed the
Malcolm X book on his desk like it was the Bible,
with one of those green ribbon page markers flaring out of the binding; how he'd pick it up period-
ically as if he had to remind himself of a certain
scripture or a holy parable. You do that a lot when
you feel yourself slipping.

In English I tried to pay attention to Mr. Savery,
but I started to daydream. I couldn't get Truvoy's
book out of my mind. I kept thinking about how
the main character went cooning in the fields, and
how it sounded kind of fun. I pictured myself
hanging out with Truvoy and Malcolm X. We'd
shoot some hoops together, order a pepperoni
pizza, tell some jokes, and teach each other how to
German Smurf and get booty.

Then, to cap the night off before it got dark,
we'd go cooning. I pictured us running through a
field with a zillion bright-green watermelons. We'd
fool the farmer with our quickness and light feet,
and pirate the biggest, fattest, juiciest ones and
stack them in a wheelbarrow.

I saw myself taking one home to Mom. She'd ask, *"Where'dya get that, Mike?"* and I'd say, *"Cooning, Mom. I went cooning with Truvoy and Malcolm X. And I had a great time."*

After class it started to rain. The clouds were all gray and aluminum-looking and the wind had kicked up pretty fierce. Over the loudspeaker, a kid said, *"Fifteen minutes first call battalion police call, fifteen minutes first call battalion police call, uniform is coveralls and gym shoes, fifteen minutes first call."*

All of a sudden, a zillion kids with red stripes on their hats started sprinting toward the barracks. I followed their cue, remembering that I had to be at formation, on the guard path at parade rest, by five minutes first call.

The sky burst open and the rain came really hard. A clap of thunder echoed over the campus, in the rocky lookout towers, and everything became very gray. Everybody on campus ran for shelter, with their books shielding their heads.

In the barracks, all of the new boys were square-cornering at hyper-speed. They looked like one of those super-fast, old black-and-white silent movies. All of the old boys in the hall said, "Post," and let me go by without a struggle.

In the room, Truvoy was rubbing lotion into his legs again. *"Ten minutes first call battalion police call, ten minutes first call battalion police call, uniform is coveralls and gym shoes, ten minutes first call. Formation is INSIDE!"* Everyone in the barracks cheered, like inside formation meant we were going to load up in vans and head for the strip bars.

"I can't believe these crazy jokers are gonna still have us totin' trash when it's rainin'. They must think we're waterproof or something," Truvoy said, massaging his calves. "I have a game this weekend. The last thing my ass needs is a *cold*. I have enough problems."

"Did you catch any flack for what happened last night?" I asked, hurrying into my coveralls.

"Catch any *flack*? Who's gonna give me flack? The last person who gave me *flack* got a *smack*."

"Oh," I said. "I just thought Nealy or someone would be breathing down your neck by now."

"That's the last place Nealy wants to breathe," Truvoy said. "You better fall out to formation. I can smell the bacon burning off Hillcrest from here." I walked out of the room and square-cornered it to the end of the hall, where all the new boys were standing at parade rest in their coveralls. I took my place at the end of the squad and fixed my hands in the small of my back. The kid over the loudspeaker came on again. *"Five minutes first call, battalion police call, five minutes first call battalion police call. Uniform is coveralls and gym shoes. Five minutes first call. Formation is inside."*

Out of the corner of my eye, I saw Truvoy slowly making his way down to formation. His posture was pretty poor, and he wasn't really marching like he was supposed to. Hillcrest was standing on the other side of the hall. Truvoy walked right past him without posting or saying *Sir, excuse me, sir.* Hillcrest didn't do anything, and all of the new boys witnessed the whole thing. Truvoy took his spot in our squad and stood at parade rest.

Hillcrest came over holding a bunch of plastic garbage bags. He cleared his throat.

"Well, my pretties," he said, "since we have a bit of a *storm* outside, Captain Wild has decided to alter our plans a bit. Because you all have been given the distinct *privilege* of temporary Silver M's next weekend, we thought we would make you earn them a little *faster*. We don't like to hand out free lunches here at good old camp SAMMA, do we, Tegroff?"

"No, sir," I said.

"So guess what? You new boy *fucks* get to do the

police call for the rest of the company. Yes, that's right, for the whole goddamn company. And I'm gonna supervise your pretty little asses. And you're gonna pick up every gum wrapper, cigarette butt, and bread crumb off the ground. I want you to dig out the grass if it's dirty. And we'll stay out there all goddamn night if we have to. I don't care if dog shit starts fallin' outta the sky. You understand me?"

We all shouted, *"Yes, sir!"*

Hillcrest turned to me. "Do you understand me, Tegroff?"

"Yes, sir!" I said, hating his guts, remembering how purple and swollen his face had looked when Truvoy had him wrapped up. He handed all of us bags and assigned partners, except for me because of the odd number. He told me that I would have to work by myself, which meant I'd have to go at it twice as hard.

Hillcrest marched us out into the rain, behind the gymnasium, where candy bar wrappers, cigarette cartons, and torn napkins stuck to the ground like wet guts. It was pretty terrible, having to touch all of that wet crap. Everything felt like soggy toilet paper.

The sky was getting darker and darker, as if a huge black quilt was looming overhead. The rain was spraying into my eyes and dripping off the end of my nose. My bag was getting heavy because of all the drenched paper.

As I bent down to pick up a fractured doughnut box, Hillcrest grabbed me and threw me to the ground. I landed on my back and crossed my arms over my head.

"What the hell are you doing, Tegroff? You *missed* this!" he yelled, digging into my bag, grabbing some sloppy garbage that I'd collected and throwing it at my face. Some of it got in my mouth. It tasted terrible, like some stray dog's intestines. I spit it out.

"Drop and give me twenty for missing that trash, Jackoff." I looked around, to see if anyone was watching. I looked for Truvoy. My stomach started knotting up.

"Now!" he screamed.

"Yes, sir," I said.

I dropped and started pumping off push-ups, counting in between each thrust. My arms were really sore and I was completely waterlogged. Rain slapped the back of my neck and rolled onto my shoulders, chilling my whole body. I felt all clammy and fishy, like I'd just crawled out of the Chicago River.

When I was done, he stood over me, holding me in position.

"You think your *nigger boyfriend's* gonna be able to protect you all the time, Tegroff? You think he's gonna walk in your shadow? You think he's gonna take showers with you and hold your hand in the shit house?"

"No, sir," I said with what little air could sneak out of my collapsing lungs.

"No, *sirrrr*," he said all feminine and sing-songy, mocking me. "You're gonna have a *long* semester, Jackoff. Nigger Boy's not gonna be there all the time. Give me ten more."

"But, sir," I said, "I-can't-do-any—"

"What the hell's goin' on here, Sergeant?" I looked up. It was Lieutenant Tomisac, the guy who'd jumped out of his pants when I dropped my books and sat on the poker by the library. Hillcrest snapped to attention.

"Disciplining a member of my unit, sir," Hillcrest said.

"In the *rain*?" Lieutenant Tomisac asked, the rain beading on his silver pips, running off onto his shoulders.

"Yes, sir," Hillcrest said. "I felt it was an appropriate punishment."

"What'd he do?" Lieutenant Tomisac asked.

"He started throwing garbage out of his bag." I never wanted a harpoon more in my life. Lieutenant Tomisac told me to get up. I heaved myself to my feet.

"Did you do that, cadet?" he asked me.

"No, sir. No, I did not. I *swear* I didn't," I said, my nose full of snot and rain.

"Well, then," Lieutenant Tomisac said, "why don't you pick up this garbage right here and go back to the barracks and dry off. Sergeant Hillcrest, why don't you drop and give me ten." Hillcrest plastered a completely dramatic look all over his face. *"Now!"* Lieutenant Tomisac screamed. "Drop now, Sergeant Hillcrest, or I'll write you up for physical hazing!"

Hillcrest looked around and quickly pumped off ten push-ups in front of Lieutenant Tomisac and me. When he was finished, Lieutenant Tomisac turned to me and winked. Hillcrest had barely made it, grunting with each count.

"Go tell Captain Wild I said you could return to the barracks. Get in some warm clothes," Lieutenant Tomisac said.

"Thank you, sir," I said, gathering my bag of trash. I was cold and soggy all over. The rain was coming down harder and the sky was getting darker and everything looked bruised. Some thunder ripped in the distance. The campus looked haunted. My coveralls were waterlogged and heavy, and I felt like I was lugging a couple of suitcases.

I turned back around for a brief moment to see what Hillcrest looked like in push-up position. Lieutenant Tomisac was saying something kind of loud, but I couldn't make it out because of all the rain and the wind kicking up.

This kid in my neighborhood, Tom Jenko, used to hang out on the corner of Rooney Drive and wait for me to get off the school bus, twisting his key leash around his fingers. He had long, black, stringy hair that looked like a nest of African snakes hissing off his head, and he always wore these completely Wild Bill Hickok–looking cowboy boots with silver tips. He also wore a pair of ratty bell-bottom jeans that had Kilroy spray-painted on his left back pocket. He was probably four years older than me, but I really couldn't make out his age because he had pits in his face and his eyes were always swollen shut. He would wait for me to walk past him. I would just ignore him and try to walk a little faster, but I could always hear his key leash jingling like a box of knives the minute I'd pass him. Then he'd put his arm around me and ask for his "goodies." He'd say, "Where are my goodies, Mickey Mouse?" and I'd hand him the measly forty-five cents that I hadn't used in the lunchroom. Then, he'd softly pat me on the back of the head a couple times and smash me a good one right in the ribs.

When I'd get home from the bus, Mom would always ask me where my change from lunch was and I'd tell her that I'd used it to play a couple of games of Pac-Man at the 7-Eleven and then I'd go lock myself in the bathroom and rub the sting out of my ribcage.

After watching Lieutenant Tomisac punish Hillcrest, I turned around to walk back to the barracks. With every step, my legs became heavier and heavier, and my coveralls were practically pulling themselves off of me. I couldn't get the thought of colliding with something out of my head. I felt like I was on that school bus all over again, and that somewhere, in one of the longer back seats, Hillcrest was on it too, licking his chops, waiting to get off with me at Rooney Drive.

chapter fifteen

Only the Lonely

I knocked myself out trying to walk up the steps in Glenwood Hall. My coveralls were soaked and my nose was still snotty and my face was pasty. I probably looked like a drug fiend who got caught in a monsoon without his crack, with my acorn hairdo pointy from the rain. I square-cornered it to Captain Wild's room and knocked on his door. Nobody was there so I knocked a few more times. Still nobody answered so I walked down to the bathroom.

I was about to walk into the bathroom when I heard some strange squishing noises coming from the shower room. It sounded like a washing machine sloshing clothes around. I pressed my ear to the steel door, and listened for a second. I heard a really strange low grunting noise and a couple of *oohs* along with the sloppy sounds. I looked down the hall to see if anyone was watching me, maybe an old boy who had an appetite for dishing out some push-ups.

Then, with a nudge from my shoulder, the door jolted open. My jaw dropped so low I thought I'd dislocated it. The room was all steamy and thick but I could see someone flopping his body around in this stain of shampoo under one of the old boy shower heads. The water was sizzling and everything was pretty muggy. The kid made this spastic attempt to spring off the ground, but slipped all over himself and practically cracked his skull open on the tile floor. Then he surrendered to all of the water and the steam and just lay there on his belly. After a few seconds, he looked up at me. It was Warner. As soon as he saw me, he slowly stood up, staring at his groin the whole time. He had an erection and his stomach was all sappy-looking from the shampoo.

I just stood there with the door open. He grabbed his towel and quickly wrapped it around his body. His face was completely red and his eyes were bulging out of his head. He walked slowly toward me with his johnson trying to poke through the towel and then kind of picked up speed. He kept looking down at his groin and trotted out of the shower room with his towel and his little sticky erection, leaving his shampoo and soap dish under the shower head like a couple of bad memories.

I eventually went to the bathroom, where I held myself between my fingers with special care, and then I made my way back to my room. I got out of my wet clothes and put on a T-shirt and some pajama bottoms. I know it's strange that I still wear pajamas, but I like to wear them around the house when I'm just winding down and trying to relax. They don't have *Star Wars* characters or the cast from *Yogi's Laugh Olympics* plastered all over them or anything like that. They're just a pair of old checkered flannel bottoms that hug me nice around the ankles. Mom bought them for me a couple of Christmases ago, when I'd asked for Nintendo. She got me this Mattel hand-held basketball game and the pajamas. The game shorted out after about a month, and I eventually grew out of the pajama top, which started to grip me in the armpits. Alice wears it as a nightshirt now. For some reason, the bottoms seemed to grow with me, to stretch in all the right places, and I've worn them ever since. I don't think I'll ever get sick of my old flannels.

After I slipped into my pajamas, I sat down at my desk. I decided to take a crack at the definition of leadership Captain Peck had assigned us in M.T. I remembered what he'd said about looking inside yourself to find the answer, so I started looking inside myself. I didn't peel my fingernails back or look down my shorts or anything pornographic. I just tried to clear my mind and think about being a leader and all of that half-baked General MacArthur crap.

Well, as I was sitting there, feeling kind of comfortable in my flannels, I started thinking about Hufford and Hillcrest and Dad and Dr. Sharifporte, and I came to the conclusion that no one could really be a leader because practically everybody's a complete bastard inside, underneath all of the stripes and fake tans and smiling mustaches and false promises. I basically came up with the idea that everyone's pretty much out for themselves.

The only people I would consider leaders are those who don't really give a damn about anything, like that kid who jumped out of the tree in the story we read in Mr. Savery's class. He didn't really care about anything, so he had nothing to gain, so he wasn't going to be tempted to screw anyone else over. I started to write that down when someone knocked on my door. It was Warner. I snapped to attention.

"At ease, Tegroff," he said. "You can sit down." He kept bobbing back and forth on the balls of his feet like he didn't know for sure whether or not he wanted to come in. He looked pretty choked up and kept pulling at his fingers.

"Back there in the shower," he said, "I know it looked pretty retarded." He cleared his throat and kept pulling at his fingers, which were starting to get all red and blotchy-looking. "I don't know why I was . . . I can't really explain what—"

"I know, sir," I said.

"Um. I'd kind of appreciate it if you wouldn't, like, tell anyone about it. I'm up for sergeant next semester and if those bastards found out, I don't think I'd—"

"I know, sir."

"I mean, you get kind of lonely here sometimes, and everything just kind of builds up inside you and you have to . . ." He was really pulling at his fingers. I thought they were going to pop off. "Well, you know what I mean." He laughed for a second but then his face fell flat.

"I know, sir. I won't say anything. I didn't see it. It's forgotten." Warner practically jumped out of his socks and plastered this really dramatic smile all over his orange cheeks.

"Great. Great. Thanks, Tegroff. And you don't have to call me *sir* anymore. I'm John. Just call me John." He walked over and extended his hand toward me. I looked at it for a second, and then shook it.

chapter sixteen
Parachutes

When Warner left, I tried to get my thoughts back on track about leadership. Every time I tried to write down what I'd been thinking before Warner walked in, my mind would get blocked. It was like a huge piece of flypaper had been crumpled and stashed in my brain. So I took a deep breath and tried to rearrange everything.

I started to think about the big weekend coming up and who'd be willing to visit me. Mom couldn't because of Alice's show, and I wasn't about to ask Dad after the stuff he and Rayne had pulled on me. So I started thinking about the one person who just might show up, the one person who might take the weekend off and hang out with me for a couple of days: Charlie Brown. I figured he had nothing better to do because of Mom being in

Philadelphia, and I thought we might even get to squeeze in a couple of games of one-on-one in between all of the parading around.

So I took out a piece of paper and started to write Charlie Brown a letter.

Dear Charlie,

I know this is probably a surprise hearing from your old one-on-one partner, but I have something to ask you. You see, I'm at this serious school where everyone thinks we're at war, and they're having this great weekend coming up where they invite all of the parents. I thought that since Mom's in Philadelphia and my dad can't make it, that you might be interested in coming up. There will probably be a lot of neat stuff planned like rappelling and the football game, and we might even get to shoot some hoops together in the field house between all the fireworks. I've been working on my jumper and it's really clicking. I don't think you'd stand much of a chance anymore. You probably won't recognize me because I got this completely demented haircut that makes me look like an acorn. It's so bad it even makes me jealous of your hair. Well, I look forward to hearing from you. It could be a fun time. Please write me back.

P.S. You can even bring your saxophone if you want.

Your Pal,
Mike

I wrote the address of Mom's work on an envelope, stuffed it, and left it on top of my desk.

I really didn't know what to do with myself because after writing the letter, and sharing that special moment with Warner, and getting my mind all jammed up, I didn't feel much like studying. You have to be in one of those moods to start calculating algebra equations and my thoughts about leadership had abandoned me. So, I don't know why, I guess out of complete boredom, I walked over to Truvoy's desk to check out his crucifix. I took it off his wall and went back to my seat. I sat there, staring at it without blinking. I could feel my eyes drying out, I was staring so hard. He looked like Jose Cardinal, an old center fielder for the Chicago Cubs.

So there I was, staring at the Black Jesus with the cross close to my face. I looked up and Truvoy was standing there in the doorway, watching me.

"You prayin'?" he asked. His coveralls were completely soaked. Water was dripping off the ends of his sleeves.

"No. I was just looking."

"What, you bugged out because you never saw a Black Jesus before?"

"Yeah. I guess I kind of *bugged* out. I always saw Jesus as this malnourished version of Santa Claus." Truvoy laughed while he pulled a T-shirt over his head. His stomach was all rippled and stony-looking.

"And I always saw him as a tired version of Jimmy Walker," he said, pulling the too-small shirt off his shoulders, "strollin' into discos with his apostles, poppin' off 'Dy-no-mite!,' thowin' black-eyed peas in the air and blessin' everybody and their sister."

"*Good times!*" I said. "They still play that on WGN in Chicago. Jimmy Walker's hilarious."

"That joker used to have me rollin'. Him and Thelma always arguin' and carryin' on. I used to watch that program like it was goin' outta style. Just to see Thelma's smokin' ass. That babe's one of the finest dishes on the menu. I'll tell you what, Thelma can sleep in my bed any day."

"Yeah," I said. "She's pretty."

He took the cross out of my hand and fixed it above his desk. Then he turned around and kind of smiled.

"You got a girl back home?" he asked.

"No, not really," I said.

"No special little thing to send you care packages?"

"Well, there's this one girl who lives on my block, but I wouldn't call her my girlfriend."

"What's her name?" Truvoy asked, smiling.

"You're gonna laugh."

"Why?"

"It's kind of a weird name."

"Well, what is it?"

"Snoopy."

"*What?*"

"Snoopy Butterhouse."

Truvoy was doubled over, laughing his head off.

"I'm not sure if that's her real name," I said. "But that's what everyone calls her. I think I heard her parents call her Millicent once when we sat in back of them in church."

"That's a messed up name, man," Truvoy said, shaking his head, still laughing. "So she looks good?"

"I think so. She has this sandy blond hair that sits on her shoulders pretty nice."

"She like *you*?"

"She had this thing for always trying to get me alone. I'd be playing basketball down the street and she'd wait for me to come home. She'd wait for hours sometimes, right on our patio."

"Whaddya mean she was always tryin' to get you *alone?*"

"She was always trying to . . ."

"Yeah . . ."

"She always wanted to show me her . . ."

"Her what?"

"Well, you know."

"No. I don't know."

"Forget it," I said, embarrassed as hell.

"What, Mike? Her stamp collection? Her wardrobe? Her athlete's foot?" I shook my head no after every stab. Then I started to kind of smile. Truvoy made his eyes really big and goofy-looking. "No. Mike, you can't be serious," he said, his teeth beaming. "She wanted to show you *that?*"

"Yeah. *That.*" We both started to crack up like a couple of cartoons.

"Damn! That's some serious shit!"

He shook his head a couple of times and then walked over to his footlocker and started massaging his calves again. "Snoopy, huh," he said, shaking his head, still laughing a little. I didn't even want to begin to tell him about Mom's boyfriend, Charlie Brown. He would have probably had a stroke or something.

Truvoy looked up at me.

"Well?" he said.

"Well, what?"

"Did you ever see it?" he asked.

"Last summer, when I was taking the trash out, she kind of cornered me in my garage by the kitty litter box, and I couldn't get away because I would have stomped on a bunch of turds and my arms were full of Hefty bags."

"She cornered you?!"

"Yeah." I was laughing pretty hard.

"So she showed it to you?"

"Yeah."

"*Damn, Mike!* What happened?!"

"I don't know. All I know is that I dropped the trash all over myself. I was practically standing in a litter box with egg cartons and cheese wrappers falling all over me."

"So then what'd you do?" Truvoy asked.

"Well, I just kind of stood there frozen for a second, and then I left—I guess I was scared."

"What you were scared of was *yourself*," Truvoy said.

I didn't say anything and started picking at my cuticles.

"You were afraid of yourself," he continued. "You were afraid to get busy 'cause you never did nothin' like that before. You wouldn't jump out of no plane without a parachute, would you?"

"I guess not."

"It's because you never done nothin' like that before."

"Have you?"

"Does McDonald's sling burgers?"

"You've . . . *gotten busy?*"

Truvoy smiled ferociously.

"How old were you?" I asked.

"Twelve."

"*Twelve.* Jezus Christmas, Truvoy, you could've been a child porn star. When I was twelve, I was still playing tag. I'd hate to see what the hell you do *now*. Weren't you nervous?"

"Of course I was, but I *had* to knock those boots, Mike."

"So, what, you concentrated on a baseball game or something?"

"Have you ever seen those commercials on TV where all the soldiers jump out of the plane, where they got packs on their backs and they're all sitting in line, waiting to jump?"

"Yeah," I said, "where they try to get you to sign up and all. The parachute commercial. With the guy at the end who says 'Morning, First Sergeant.'"

"That's the one. Well, for some reason, I thought about that commercial. I thought about parachutes. And somewhere in my mind I jumped out of a plane without one."

"Wow."

"Man, I was flyin'," he said, extending his arms like the wings of a plane, his huge palms flashing.

"Parachutes," I said.

"You see, my man, when you get spooked about something, picture that plane in the back of your mind, and think about jumping. Lose the parachute. You gotta take a chance every once in a while. Just make sure that when you do, that you jump like a jackrabbit. It's not the falling that's scary. It's where you might land that can knock you out the box."

chapter seventeen

The Softest Blue

I sorted out the things in my closet before study hours. I couldn't seem to find my low-quarter shoes.

"Truvoy, have you seen my low quarters?"

"No, sir," he said jokingly. I'd practically torn my whole closet apart. All my uniforms had fallen off their hangers.

"Man. I swear they were in here," I said. "I really gotta have them. The last thing I need is to lose those bastards."

I looked under my bed, under the sink, in my desk drawers, and even under my pillow. They were gone.

"If I was you, I'd go tell Captain Wild. Someone could've boosted those jokers when you were totin' trash."

"I don't know," I said. "I don't feel too crazy

about telling the Captain that I screwed up and all. He'd probably pluck my eyebrows or drain all the blood out of me."

"Well," Truvoy said, "I hope they turn up before tomorrow morning. You can't go to formation in your slippers. Hillcrest will eat you up like a piece of candy."

During study hours, I started to look at the picture of Alice and I got to thinking about her and Mom again. I started to wonder about when I would see them again.

I started doodling, which I like to do sometimes to relax and think. I pictured my mountaintop like I did in the stairwell of Glenwood Hall on my first day, when I was looking out the window. I pictured all of the clouds and my goat and the piano. Everything was really green like in *The Sound of Music* when Julie Andrews opens her arms and sings on the top of the world. And in my mind I walked over to the piano and put my hands on the lid like I actually wanted to play. I ran my fingertips across its smooth lacquer surface, but I couldn't quite get myself to open it up. The goat came over and sat by the bench, like a dog would sit, only it was a goat, and I knew it was a goat because there was this tin can on the ground that I could tell he'd been chomping on. He sat there like he was waiting for me to play something. I looked over at my goat and he smiled the way a goat can smile when he's feeling pretty comfortable, and he *baa*ed this really nice *baa*, and we looked all cloudy together on my mountaintop, and everything became pretty lightweight and I felt like I had feathers in my brain.

I heard the clock gong in the distance a couple of times, which pulled me off my mountain. I looked down at what I'd drawn and practically flipped my lid. It was a picture of a fish with really big lips smoking a cigar. It looked like a pretty demented fish, like it was the pet of one of those spooky guys who hangs out by the Ferris wheel and watches little girls eat cotton candy. I know that's not really possible, but that's what it reminded me of.

So I was sitting there, staring at my new creation, when Hillcrest walked in the room. I snapped to attention. He was standing in the doorway, holding a pair of black low-quarter shoes. Truvoy slowly brought himself to stand at attention, and slumped to the side like he'd lost his backbone.

"Tegroff," Hillcrest said without an expression

on his face, "these were found in the trash. Someone said they were yours, as I can tell by their lackluster shine." He threw them to me one at a time. After I'd snagged both of them, I looked down at my shoes. My low quarters were completely scuffed. The bases had been raked off. I knew they were mine because they were still pretty stiff and new-looking.

"I would like you to report to the shower room in five minutes with your polish and some cotton balls. You will not leave the showers until the shine is back on them. All over them. I want glass."

"Sir," I said, "what about study hours?"

"You will shine them until I see glass. Do you understand me, Tegroff?"

"Yes, sir," I said. I just hoped a party of Louisville Sluggers wasn't awaiting me in the shower room.

"Five minutes," Hillcrest said, leaving the room.

There was a certain quiet about his face that I didn't feel too crazy about. I mean, up until then, he'd been all dramatic and snarly and fat, calling me "Jackoff" and oinking at everything, but he was calm and spooky-looking this time.

I grabbed my polish, my shoes, and a few cotton balls, and started to leave the room.

"Watch your back," Truvoy said. "If things don't feel right, get the fuck out of that shower room. Hear me? If you feel funny at all, you get the fuck out. If I was you, I'd keep the door open. All you gotta do is yell my name, and I'm there."

I nodded back to him and walked out of the room.

When I got to the shower room, Hillcrest was there by the door. He nudged the door open with his heavy shoulder and followed me in. There was a shower head that was dripping slowly, like an old clock ticking and tocking. I held everything kind of close to my chest to act as a shield just in case Hillcrest started throwing karate chops at me.

"Sit down, Tegroff," he said, staring at the dripping shower head, not even looking me in the eyes. The floor was cold and clammy. Not all the water had evaporated from the previous shower. I felt like I was in a concentration camp.

"Start polishing."

I pulled out a cotton ball, twisted the lid off the polish, dampened my cotton ball in one of the drops that was leaking, squeezed the extra water out, rubbed the cotton ball full of black wax, and started making reverse zeros into my dingy, scuffed shoes.

"I want glass," Hillcrest said quietly, still staring off at the shower head.

"Yes, sir," I said, driving reverse zeros into my low quarters.

Hillcrest slowly turned around and started to leave. His feet shuffled while he turned like he was really tired, like when you wake up in the middle of the night and you want to make yourself a peanut butter and jelly sandwich and you can't really get your legs going because they're still asleep. He wedged the door shut behind him.

After he left, I just sat there for a second and watched the rusty shower head drip all over the place. I thought about how sorry everything was again: how I was sitting on my ass in a community shower, shining my shoes like someone in a loony bin.

I started to think about how things in general are all pretty loony, like the bit about Warner humping the floor that I was shining my shoes on, and how my shoes had suddenly gotten lost and scuffed, and how my shoulders were sore as hell, and how I was starting to feel tired, and how I hadn't played basketball since Hufford had blasted me in the ear, and for some reason, I associated all of that stuff with that sad shower head that kept dripping, and

I stood up and went over to it and grabbed the handle and tried to make it stop. I forced it up toward the off arrow, but it kept dripping. I positioned my body under it so I could use my legs. I could feel my arms shaking. The handle was about as tight as it could get, but for some reason, I kept driving up with all my might, but it wouldn't budge. Some retarded plumber hadn't hooked it up right, and that just about drove me crazy. I just wanted to sit there and think about things without having to watch that nozzle crying all over the place.

I started shouting at it.

"STOP DRIPPING, DAMMIT!" I didn't recognize my voice.

"JACKASS SONUVABITCHIN' JOKER."

"HE AIN'T DONE NOTHIN'!" I screamed.

"HE AIN'T DONE NOTHIN' TO YOU!!"

The steel handle started cutting into the meat of my palm. I stopped and kicked the wall, and that was pretty stupid because I didn't have any shoes on.

After a while, I sat back down and started shining my shoes again. I rubbed about two coats of polish into the tips and a new base started to form. I'd used a couple of cotton balls and I was down to my last one. After a while, the cotton starts to get hard and wiry and scratches the surface of your shine, so you have to be careful and use new ones every fifteen or twenty minutes.

When the last one hardened, I got up, nudged the door with my hip. I peered down the hallway to make sure Hillcrest was out of sight, and walked back to my room to ask Truvoy if I could borrow some cotton balls. I made sure to square-corner it pretty fast.

When I got to my room, my door was closed and I could hear some muffled voices. I was pretty sure that one of them was Hillcrest's, but I wasn't sure about the others. I heard Truvoy say something about "letting me be" and then I heard this other kid say something about "not having any dumb niggers in Echo Company." It was First Sergeant Nealy. I pressed my ear to the door, and all of the sudden, all of this stuff sounded like it was flying all over the room. I heard a desk drawer slam shut, and the sound bodies make when they land on carpeting. Truvoy made some terrible noises like he was getting hurt. I heard a couple of grunts, and the deep, clothes-muffled noise that fists make when they drive into someone's body. Then Truvoy groaned and said, *"Please stop,"* but they kept doing whatever they were doing, and he kept making terrible noises, pleading like a child.

My body froze there at the door. My joints completely stiffened up, and I couldn't breathe very well. My hand was on the doorknob. I wanted to turn it. I wanted to open it up and throw myself into the room and help him, but something inside me wouldn't let me; something inside me told me to run, so I pushed myself away from the door and I started to run down the hall. I sprinted down the hall and ran down the stairs. I slammed through the doors of Glenwood Hall, and just kept running. It was really dark out and the rain was cold. The only thing I could really make out were the lights shining through the stained glass windows in the chapel. I was hyperventilating like crazy, and my head felt like it was going to explode and my heart was blasting out of my chest.

For some reason, I headed for the chapel. I really don't know why, but the purplish lights from the windows looked kind of safe, so I kept running toward them. Leaves were shooting out from under my feet. It was raining and the sky was all charcoaly and I could feel it falling on top of me.

When I reached the chapel doors, I stopped running and gasped for breath at the entrance. Organ music was filling the incensed air, and all of the candles in the alcoves were shooting little shadows onto the rocky walls. All of the pews were empty. The only person in the chapel was the old Italian lady. She was playing the organ. The music was really loud and sad. Her eyes were closed and her body writhed with the slow parts. My legs were all rubbery, and I thought I was going to collapse.

I lurched down the aisle between the pews and watched the old lady working the organ. The music sounded really sad, and all of the harmony started to make everything slow down. I kept walking toward the lady. I had to push off one of the pews to keep my balance. For some reason, all I wanted to do was get close to the organ and kind of sit there.

The music started to make me feel really tired, and I remember getting to the altar and really struggling to get up the steps so I could get to the organ. When the lady saw me, she stopped playing and got up from her bench and walked toward me. I dropped to my knees. The pain of hitting the rocky floor shot up my legs, but I didn't care. It didn't matter. I remember how blue her polyester pants were when she stood in front of me, and for some reason, the blue in her pants seemed like the most important thing in the world. I grabbed her around the legs and pulled her close.

chapter eighteen

Magic Markers

When I woke up, Mr. Savery was standing over me. I was in a little white room. My bed was layered in thick, sterile sheets. My old flannels were bunched up in my groin and my legs felt kind of tingly and sandy from my pajamas twisting up. My mouth tasted pasty, like I'd pounded a bottle of Elmer's glue.

A ribbon of sunlight streamed in through a small window on the other side of the room. I could see little particles of dust sparkling through the light.

"How ya feelin', partner?" Mr. Savery asked. He was holding a briefcase and his hair was slick from a shower. He looked like he was on his way to class.

"Where am I?"

"You're in the infirmary," he said. "You collapsed last night. I think they want you to take it easy for a day or two." He sat down at the end of the bed. "You know, running around in your pajamas like that would scare the Christmas out of most old women. You're lucky Mrs. Notali doesn't get spooked easily."

"How'd I get here?" I asked. My head was throbbing, and I had to go to the bathroom.

"The security guard carried you across campus. He said for being thin, you must have cement in your pants. I told him that ball players always carry their weight well."

I didn't say anything.

A nurse walked in with a thermometer and a blood pressure unit. She was really short and chubby, but a nice kind of chubby. She looked like someone's sweet old Aunt Louise.

"Hi, Mike," she said. "How are you feeling?" She rolled up my sleeve and started to strap the black band around my arm.

"I don't know," I said. "I guess my head kind of throbs, and a couple of Cokes wouldn't hurt." She started pumping the little rubber ball and my arm got thick.

"How have you been eating?" she asked, letting a little air hiss out.

"I don't know," I said. "I guess I don't really pay

attention. I just mostly eat whatever's on the menu."

"You haven't been eating," she said, reading the little gauge by the balloon. "Have you ever fainted before?"

"Well," I said, "once when this kid from my neighborhood got in a motorcycle accident and his arms were all crusty and bloody. My knees got a little weak but I didn't keel over or anything."

"But you've never actually *fainted* before?" she asked, slipping a digital thermometer into my mouth.

"You've never passed out at a wedding or anything like that?" Mr. Savery asked. I shook my head no. "You didn't even get *dizzy* when the Bulls lost that triple overtimer in the finals last year?" I shook my head again. "I nearly lost my cookies. Made me wanna run off to the woods and start my life over."

I smiled with the thermometer in my mouth.

"Well," the nurse said, pulling the beeping thermometer out of my mouth, "you don't have a fever, and your b.p. is normal, but we're gonna keep you here till dinner. You need to get some rest. I think along with your poor eating habits, you have a pretty bad case of the six-thirty reveille blues. Your body's not used to getting up before the rest of the world."

"Yeah," I said. "I guess I haven't been sleeping that great lately."

"I'll bring you some breakfast in about twenty minutes. You have your choice of scrambled eggs, fried eggs, or poached eggs," she said, her chubby arms wiggling as she reached for a pen and pad of paper off the bedside stand.

"Oatmeal?"

"Now there's a man who's out to win my heart," Mr. Savery said. "The hearty man's meal. Mix in a little maple syrup and you got some serious rib-sticking going on."

"Yesiree," the nurse said, "oatmeal it is. Toast and jelly, too?"

"Oatmeal with sugar and butter," I said.

"Okay," the nurse said, "but I'm gonna bring you some toast and jelly, too. And if you don't promise me you'll eat it up I'll keep ya in here till tomorrow."

"Cinnamon toast?" I pleaded.

"Okay," she said, wagging the thermometer at me, "but you gotta eat it."

"I promise."

When she left the room, Mr. Savery opened his briefcase and handed me a piece of paper.

"Here," he said, handing it to me, "this is the schedule for tryouts. What's your shoe size?" he asked, flipping open a folder with a bunch of numbers on it.

"I think it's ten, but my foot keeps growing. Better go with ten and a half."

"Good idea. Play it safe. That'll give you some room for an extra pair of socks. Keeps blisters away."

He closed his folder and slid it back into his briefcase. Nothing was said for a minute or two. I just watched the dust gliding on the line of sunlight that was starting to angle up the wall.

"Is everything all right, Mike?" he asked. I nodded my head. "Because I can't be having one of my crack playmakers bailing out on me. That's like losing the anchor off a ship. The team will start drifting out to sea." I just kept staring at the dusty twinkles in the light. I wasn't blinking for some reason. I could feel my eyes starting to dry out.

"Is there something you'd like to talk about?" he asked.

"No. Not really."

"You can talk to me, Mike. I want to help." The light was starting to fill the room. It hurt my eyes if I looked directly into it.

"I guess I'm not feeling too crazy about being here, that's all," I said.

I looked at him for a moment, but nothing

seemed to want to come out. He nodded his head a couple of times and smiled. Then he took a deep breath and sat down at the end of my bed.

"You know, when I was growing up, my dad used to come home with all of these markers that he'd bring from his office. He was a foreman at a tool and dye factory so he could get a lot of office supplies for free. And he'd always bring me home different-colored markers, and I would draw with them and collect them. It wasn't so important that I used them as it was that I had them. Sometimes I'd just hold onto the coffee can that I kept them in and look at all the colors. Just because. I guess it would make me think of my father."

His face went blank for a second.

"Well, one night, when I was fifteen, he didn't come home. We thought he'd just stopped off to play some pool with his buddies. I didn't think about it and went to my friend's house to play some three-on-three. Later that night we got a call," he said. His voice started to get kind of quiet. "He'd had a heart attack on his way home from work." Mr. Savery had to take a couple of breaths and look at his hands. "When they brought us his belongings, there was a rubber band wrapped around all of these new colored markers. Pink and orange and green. He hadn't brought a marker home in years. I was fifteen. What the heck was I going to do with a magic marker, anyway? But he'd had them in his back pocket. He'd remembered. For a long time, I had a pretty hard time with my father passing away. I was sixteen and I'd lock myself in my room and draw pictures with my markers like I was still a little kid.

"Finally," he said, "I started talking about it with this woman at my high school, and it really helped. There's something about getting it all out that heals you. Letting the poison out. You can't go around pent up. It catches up to you. Like one of those lightning-fast point guards with magic hands. He's gonna steal the ball from you one time during the game, and you know it. You just don't know when." He shook his head a couple of times. "So just remember, Mike, if there's something you'd like to talk about, I'm always here for you. Just remember that. I look out for my ball players."

I looked at him and smiled. For some reason, all that stuff about his dad kicking the bucket with those magic markers in his back pocket made me feel a little better.

Mr. Savery took another deep breath.

"Well," he said, "I gotta go talk to my sophomores

about blowing off their journal entries. Is there anything I can getcha? The sports section? A cinnamon roll? Vanna White?"

"Bridget Fonda," I said, smiling.

"Well, I'll work on her. I'll get on the phone to her agent after lunch. But anything in the meantime?"

"Can you play the saxophone?" I asked.

"No, but I can play a pretty mean guitar." We both laughed. My head was starting to feel a lot better. "When you get out of here, if you feel like talking again, just stop by."

"OK."

"Check out that tryout schedule," he said, turning to leave. "And rest well."

"I will," I said, feeling like things were starting to sort themselves out. "Thanks, Mr. Savery."

I was eight years old the last time I stayed in a hospital. I had to get my tonsils removed. Mom, Dad, and Alice all came to visit me at the same time. Dad was pretty nervous and kept clearing his throat, but he settled down after Alice crawled up in bed with me and sang "Smile, Darn Ya, Smile" into a plastic fork. I remember that Dad had his arm around Mom, pulling her close, and Mom had her head on his shoulder. At that time, they'd been divorced for two years. Alice always had a knack for pulling everything together.

I think that was the last time I actually saw Mom and Dad within three feet of each other.

Some time passed and then the nurse returned with my food. She adjusted my bed so I could sit upright, and placed the tray on my lap.

"There's someone here to see you, Mike," she said. She handed me a couple of napkins. I looked at the doorway. Dad was standing there with his briefcase, leaning against the wall.

"I'll leave you two alone," the nurse said as she turned to leave.

"Hi, Michael," Dad said.

"Hi, Dad."

"How do you feel?"

I shrugged my shoulders.

"I like your hair," he said, smiling carefully. I faked a smile and looked down toward my feet at the end of my bed.

"You all right, Michael?"

"I'm tired, OK?" I tried to put a piece of toast in my mouth, but I couldn't because I felt like I was going to cry. I put the toast down.

"I used to wear my hair like that when I was your age. The girls like that style. You'll be knockin' em dead."

I didn't reply. I couldn't look at him. I clamped my teeth together hard. My jaws were locked. Dad took a step forward and adjusted his pants.

"They called me at home last night," he said, looking at the backs of his hands. "What happened?"

"Oh, nothing much really." I was having a little trouble talking. I could feel the tears coming, but I fought them off as best as I could.

"Nothing much doesn't put you in the hospital, Michael."

I concentrated on my breathing. I just wanted air to keep coming in and out of my chest.

"Not eating enough, huh?" he said.

"Yeah, right."

He leaned his back against the wall and took a deep breath.

"Son, Rayne and I had a long talk this morning."

"About what?" I asked. Dad walked over and sat at the end of my bed. He put his hand on my arms and rubbed my shoulder. I pulled away.

"You," he said.

I squeezed my eyes shut as hard as I could.

"I told her I wanted you to come home at the end of the semester if things don't work out here. Would you like that?"

I nodded my head. I tried not to look at him. A lump started to form in my throat. I kept staring at this velvet picture of a clown with balloons in his cheeks. There was a small spider climbing up the frame. We didn't say anything to each other for a while.

Dad walked back and forth across the room. After a few minutes he stopped in front of the picture of the clown. He stared at it for a moment and then he lifted his hand and started touching the balloons in the clown's cheeks.

"Dad?"

"Yes, Michael?"

"Are you doing anything special next weekend?"

Dad started wringing his hands together. Then he twisted his wedding band a couple of times.

"Well, Rayne and I were planning on going to Vermont to visit her parents. Why?"

"It's just that there's this big weekend here, that's all. And I can have a visitor."

"Well, we'll see," he said. "We've been planning this trip for a long time. But I'll see what I can do. I'll talk to Rayne, OK?"

"OK."

He rubbed his hand through my hair. It felt nice.

"I miss you, sport."

I nodded and tried to swallow the swelling in my throat. My face got hot and I started to cry. I tried not to but I couldn't keep it back anymore. I pulled Dad's arm into my chest with all my might.

"I love you, Michael. I really do." He put his head on my shoulder and for a moment it seemed like he was crying himself. He stayed there for a few minutes and I touched his hair.

After a while he got up and rubbed his face with one of my napkins.

"I'm really proud of you for giving this a shot, Michael." He stood there for a minute or so and then he grabbed his briefcase.

"I better get going," he said. "Rayne's expecting me."

"You should see me do push-ups, Dad," I said. "I think I'm getting a lot stronger."

"That's great, Mike. I used to do a lot of push-ups when I was your age. In sets of ten. They're good for your chest."

He rubbed the front of his briefcase. Then he started rummaging through one of his jacket pockets.

"Hey, I got you these," he said, pulling out a set of purple wristbands. "They'll match your uniform." When he offered them to me I noticed how big and meaty his hands were. I'd never really noticed that before.

"Thanks," I said, pulling them out of their plastic wrapping.

"OK then," Dad said. "I'll call the Commandant's office and let you know about next weekend."

I nodded. Dad turned to leave. I watched him go like he was part of a dream.

chapter nineteen
A Little Cracker

I guess I ate myself to sleep. When I woke up, I had oatmeal all over my face and a blob of buttery cinnamon stuck to my ear.

I never thought I could get that tired. I'd been really zapped before, like after one of those practices where Coach would make us run gut drills because our center who had bad ankles had missed a lay-up, but this was a different kind of tired. This was a Rip Van Winkle tired; when your bones get run down and the whole bit. My hair even felt sleepy.

I yawned a couple of times and started to pick the dried oatmeal off my face when the nurse came back in with a washcloth.

"Hey, Sleepyhead. Your friend's here to see ya. All these visitors," she said, washing the cinnamon off my ear. "I'm gonna have to start warding them off so you can get some rest." Then she looked down at my tray. "You didn't finish your oatmeal."

"I know," I said, "I guess I kind of slept with it."

"That's OK," she said, laughing. "At least you slept a little."

Truvoy appeared at the door. His left eye was swollen shut. It looked like a pizza roll. His lower lip was also puffy-looking on the left side. The whole left side of his face looked big and cartoony, like he was half-Muppet. Dark brown surrounded his eye and mouth. The dinosaur started doing jumping jacks in my stomach again. The nurse finished cleaning me up and left us alone.

Truvoy slumped into the room with a pair of my coveralls in his hands. His face looked hard and angry.

"What's up, Crazy Eights?" he said through his swollen lip.

"Crazy who?" I asked.

"Mr. Savery came by the room. He told me you fell out last night. In the chapel."

"Yeah," I said, staring at his bad eye. "I guess I kind of freaked out."

"Now, what kind of joker's gonna be dancin' around campus in his night clothes? You musta been shinin' your shoes in that shower too long.

The smell of the polish started foolin' with your mind."

I didn't say anything. I couldn't look at his face. "What?" he said. "Cat's got your tongue?" I still couldn't say anything. "Talk to me, man," he said, placing my coveralls on the end of the bed.

"Your eye," I said. I couldn't get myself to actually ask what happened because I would have felt like a complete fake. Looking at his face just reminded me of what a coward I was.

"My *eye*," he said, "my whole *face*." The light was now pouring into the room, shining off the sheets.

"Those jackasses got me good," he continued. "They got me. I have to hand it to them. And Hillcrest's fat ass is a lot stronger than I thought."

He started rubbing his hands together.

"That's OK, though," he said. "I have something in store for their double-teaming faggot asses. The panther always roars louder after it's first bitten."

"Your lip looks like an inner tube," I said.

"Well, my man, niggas is *supposed* to have big lips, ain't they, *massa?*" he said, mocking Kunta Kinte, and sort of smiling the whole time. His whole face looked lopsided. I couldn't smile back at his comment. My face just kind of froze.

"What's wrong, Mike?" he asked. "On the serious tip. What happened last night?"

"Don't you think I should be the one asking *you* that?" I said, shifting in my bed. "You look like you just got back from Vietnam."

"I have something in store for those pussy jack-asses Nealy and Hillcrest. One at a time. They think the fireworks have cooled off just because they fucked my face up, but my vision is *fine*."

He pulled a bottle of pills out of his pocket.

"You see these? Nurse says they're supposed to make the swelling go down. Make the pain go away."

Then he shook his head and jiggled the bottle of pills a couple of times so it sounded like a rattlesnake. He threw them in the trash can by the door.

"The only medicine I need is a little revenge." He licked his wounded lip.

"Truvoy," I said. "I'm not so sure that would be such a good idea. I mean, you know how those bastards can twist things around to make you look like the bad guy because . . ." I had to catch myself. "Well, you know, because you're . . ."

"Black? A *nigga?*"

"I didn't say that, Truvoy."

"So, because I'm a *midnight special, spearchuckin' jigaboo* means that those white jackasses are gonna skate on smooth ice and I'm gonna have to live with this bullshit," he said, pointing to his sealed eye. "That might be how it works here in *St. Matty Land*, but in my book I say *fuck* that. This shit's been happenin' for too long and no one seems to wanna do shit about it."

His good eye started to glare. I kept thinking about my hand on the doorknob and how I wanted my wrist to turn ever so slightly to the left, but for some reason it wouldn't; for some terrible reason I ran like a coward.

"Truvoy," I said softly, unable to look at him in his only eye, "I was there last night. I was outside the door." I swallowed some air a couple of times. "I went back to the room. To ask you for some cotton balls. And I heard what was going on." My voice started to get shaky. I had to fake a cough. "All I wanted to do was ask you for some cotton balls." My neck started to get thick and I could feel my lip starting to quiver. "All I wanted was a couple of lousy cotton balls. Those bastards."

"Damn, Mike. *That's* why you ran off to the chapel? What, you thought God was gonna save my black ass? You thought the *white almighty* would spit a couple of lightning bolts down on those punks?"

"I don't know. I don't know why I went there. I guess it was the light."

"The what?"

"The light. All of that purple coming off the windows. And the organ music. I don't know."

"Man, you *are* crazy. *You're* the one who needs some saving grace."

"I wanted to help you. I did. But I couldn't. Everything got all paralyzed."

"Well, you're one lucky white boy, 'cause Hillcrest would have popped you in his mouth like an hors d'oeuvre, like a little white cracker with some of his sweet, sweet jam on it."

"Well, now I'm a loon. Just call me *Crazy Eights* from now on."

Truvoy laughed a little. "Crazy Eight and a *Half* if you ask me," he said. I couldn't really laugh along because of the way his face looked. He started looking at his hands and things got pretty quiet for a minute.

"Well," he said eventually, "I gotta go get that medicine."

chapter twenty
Medicine

After my blood pressure and temperature were checked again, the nurse finally let me go. Before she would sign me out, though, she made me promise her that I'd eat three square meals with all the food groups and to get to bed by taps every night. I'd try to eat all right, but I couldn't tell her that looking at Hillcrest didn't make it easy.

Back in my room, I placed my new wristbands in my top drawer and finally changed out of my coveralls and old flannels into my class grays. That's a pretty refreshing feeling: getting the heck out of some pajamas that have been bunching up in your crotch for a whole day.

I looked around for my shoes and then I remembered that I'd left them in the shower room before I'd bolted to the chapel the night before. Since all of the old boys were at formation, I blew off my square corners and jogged down to the shower room. I heaved my shoulder into the door, and it crashed open. I looked all over the place, but the only thing I could see was that rusty shower head dripping on the floor.

I decided to wear my Air Jordans, since I really had no other black shoes. I grabbed them out of my closet and sat down at my desk to put them on. While I was tying them, I noticed that Truvoy's book wasn't on his desk. I walked over and rooted through all of his books, but I couldn't find it. I even opened his drawers and looked, but there was nothing but a bunch of underwear that could have passed for Speedo swimsuits, with all of these crazy leopardskin patterns and bull's-eye symbols where your johnson is; like Truvoy thinks some horny babe is actually hunting him down with a set of bow and arrows. The book was nowhere to be found. I even hoisted up the lid of his footlocker, but there was nothing but lotion and cotton balls.

I felt like something that was mine had been taken away from me. I know it wasn't really *mine*, but it had been nice to pick it up every once in a while and read about Malcolm X and his cooning adventures.

□ □ □

Walking down to the cafeteria, I heard the cadence drums thumping away. I stopped in the stairwell to watch all of the companies marching to the mess hall. Delta looked pretty good, I thought. There was Hillcrest with his fat tan, Warner digging his left heel into the ground, looking completely serious, and Captain Wild off to the left with his pips glinting on his shoulders like silver dollars.

I looked for Truvoy, but he wasn't in the platoon. Usually, he'd be pretty easy to spot because he kind of strutted when he marched. I couldn't see him anywhere.

I made sure to wait until after announcements to enter the cafeteria. I didn't want to make a surprise appearance in the middle of announcements, wearing a pair of Air Jordans. Everyone probably knew that I'd been cooped up in the infirmary for temporarily losing my marbles. So I waited until the first couple of tables were in line and I tried to blend in with the crowd.

When I appeared at my table, my squad sized me up and down as if I'd just returned from a war with a wooden leg. All of their glances kind of stuck at the level of my shoes. They probably thought that the medical way of dealing with recovered loonies was to prescribe soft sneakers so they don't flip out and start kicking everybody in the ribs. The only person who didn't seem interested was Hillcrest, who just stared straight ahead.

"Sir," I said, "new cadet Tegroff requests permission to be seated at the table, sir."

"Sit," Hillcrest said in a sleepy voice. No one said anything to anyone else. Everyone just seemed strangely subdued. Truvoy's spot was vacant.

"Sergeant Hillcrest, sir, cadet recruit Tegroff requests permission to ask a question, sir."

"Permission granted," Hillcrest said.

"Where's cadet Shockley?" I asked. Hillcrest looked at me for a second and then looked off into space like he didn't hear me.

"Where is he, sir?" I asked again. Hillcrest wouldn't answer so I turned to Warner.

"Where's Truvoy?"

Warner looked at me sheepishly and cleared his throat. He looked all around at the table.

"Something happened—"

"As you were, Warner!" Hillcrest shouted. Everything was silent again.

I got up from the table and ran out of the cafeteria.

❑ ❑ ❑

Back in the room, all of Truvoy's clothes were strewn over his bed, next to his leather clothing bag. Truvoy was pulling things out of his drawers and putting them in his footlocker.

"Hi," I said catching my breath.

"What's up?" he replied, balling up a pair of socks.

"What's going on?" I asked. "Why are you packing?"

Truvoy didn't reply and kept balling up his socks.

"They transferring you again?"

"Yeah," Truvoy said, "I guess you could say that."

"Where to?"

"Let's just say we probably won't be roommates for a while."

"What does that mean?" I asked.

"That means they're taking me to the bus station in about twenty minutes. They kicked me out, Mike."

"They can't kick you out!"

"I guess you didn't hear."

"Hear about what?"

"Nealy."

"What'd you do, Truvoy?"

"I got that medicine," he said calmly, putting more stuff in his footlocker.

"What happened?" I asked.

"It's not important."

"Tell me!" I shouted.

"I caught up with him outside the school buildings. You shoulda seen his eyes. Nealy was one *spooked* white boy."

"What'd you do to him, Truvoy?"

"I lost control of my hands, Mike."

"Jesus."

He started balling his socks faster and faster and then he stopped, crossed his arms and looked out the window. He stared out the window for a minute or two, speechless. Then he turned and looked at me.

"They took him to a hospital in Milwaukee."

"A hospital?"

"I broke his collarbone, Mike."

"Why didn't you tell the Commandant what the hell happened?! About them double-teaming you and all!"

Truvoy shook his head no.

"Why not?!"

"Because, Mike, it would have happened sooner or later anyways. If it wasn't Nealy and Hillcrest, it would've been someone else. My black ass doesn't belong here. It's as simple as that. I'm just foolin' myself tryin' to be a part of all this *white* Uncle Sam military bullshit. It would have broke my back sooner or later. Probably sooner. And I'm not going out like that."

He walked over to the medicine chest and removed some other things.

"I'll just go back to public school," he said, packing them into the footlocker. "It ain't the end of the world."

For some reason, to me at least, it did feel like the end of the world. I didn't really know what to say. I just watched him gather his things. He took his crucifix off the wall and put it in his footlocker and walked over to his bed and stuffed all of the clothes into the clothing bag. Then he walked over to his closet and started to change out of his class grays.

"I guess I won't be needing these anymore," he said, holding his shoes, laughing a little. I laughed too, even though it wasn't really funny. "You can have them if you want," he said, facing the closet. "It'll be nice to walk around in some damn sneakers for a change. I got bunions on my toes the size of Tater Tots from those hard-ass, nonfittin', heavy jackasses." He laughed again even harder, and then he kind of stopped, and then started laughing again, really hard this time, all by himself. "You shoulda seen the look on Nealy's face," he said, cracking himself up in the closet. "The jackass looked so scared I thought he was gonna shit his pants." Now he was really letting loose. His shoulders were bobbing up and down out of control.

He was laughing so hard that it didn't really sound like laughter.

Then he stopped and took a deep breath, and his hands rose to his face. I could see his bright palms reaching up to his eyes, and, just like that, he started to softly cry. He dropped down to his knees and cried into his hands like a child. I walked over to him and put my palm on his shoulder. I felt myself getting kind of choked up too, but I did my best to fight it off because if we both had been crying, everything would have gotten sloppy and half-baked, so I just stood over his back with my hand on his shoulder.

"It ain't that bad, Mike," he said. "It *ain't*." I patted him on the back.

Then he turned and hugged me around the knees.

"You're my boy, Mike Tegroff," he said. "My *boy*."

I looked down. His swollen left eye was streaming tears. He squeezed me around the knees even harder. "My *boy!*"

I helped him carry his stuff down to a van that was waiting for him in front of Spalding Hall. We heaved his footlocker and clothing bag down the steps. The van had steel security meshing that separated the cab from the back seats.

Outside, the sky was starting to get dark like it was going to rain again. Everything looked gray. An old man with a security badge opened the back door to the van and Truvoy and I placed his stuff in it.

Truvoy still looked pretty sad, with his swollen eye and face all busted up and a couple of salty streaks dried into his cheeks. We really didn't say anything to each other. He patted me on the shoulder and smiled and then I patted him back. Then he reopened the back door of the van and unzipped his clothing bag.

"Here," he said. "I almost forgot to give you this."

He handed me his Malcolm X book.

"I know you've been reading it. Always losing my goddamn place," he said, smiling.

I smiled and took the book in my hands.

"Take it easy, Mike," he said. "Be even."

Then, I don't know why, but I walked into his arms and hugged him. I didn't want to let go. There was something about his arms that felt really safe. I could smell cocoa butter.

Eventually, I let go of him. Truvoy boarded the van and the engine started. After a minute the van disappeared through the iron gates, just like that; just like a magic trick.

I sat down on the steps of Spalding Hall and opened the book. On the inside of the cover, Truvoy had written a letter:

Dear Mike,

Work on that German Smurf. Let me know when you get your first batch of booty. Watch your back.

Your boy, —T.

He left his address in Detroit at the bottom of the page.

chapter twenty-one

Telephone Poles

Walking off campus probably wasn't very smart, but the last place I wanted to go was back to the mess hall to sit with my squad. I *thought* I was going to go back to my room, but when I reached Glenwood Hall I could see a public road running along the back of campus, where the cadet store was. Before I knew it, I was heading toward the road.

To reach it, I had to walk across a vacant parking lot with old weeds poking through the cracks. It was about fifty yards long but it felt like the length of four football fields. The edge of the other side of the parking lot was walled off with a chain link fence. Someone had spray-painted SAVE ME OLD SHIRLEY across the middle of it, and someone else had obviously tried to clean it off, but they hadn't done a very good job. It was that AWOL fence that Hillcrest had warned me about my first day. There was a piece of blue fabric stuck to the top of it that looked like a souvenir from someone's coveralls.

I threw Truvoy's book over the fence and started to climb. I was glad that I was wearing my Jordans because my low quarters were so heavy, and the clodhoppers probably wouldn't have fit through the spaces in the fence. When I got to the top, I had to lift my legs so they wouldn't catch. My pants caught on the jagged links, and I scraped my knee. After I climbed down the other side, I grabbed the book and started to walk on the shoulder of the road. The wind started to kick up again and rain started to fall.

I took my hat off in fear that someone in a car would recognize me as a cadet in my class grays and report me back to St. Matthew's. For some reason, I felt less conspicuous without the hat on.

To my right, a long cornfield stretched off into the horizon. In the distance, there were a few old clapboard houses settling into the fields. Leaves and stray garbage were whipping across the pavement of the road in mini-tornadoes.

Telephone poles towered over me like the skeletons of monsters. I started counting them to keep my mind clear. I would pass one and say the number over and over again until I'd come to the next one. "One-one-one-one-one-one-one-one-one, two-two-two-two-two-two-two-two-two," and so on.

After about thirty telephone poles, I started to realize the weight of the situation I had just put myself in.

A few cars passed but they didn't seem interested in me. I started to jog along the shoulder. The clouds seemed to be scrambling overhead. I kept thinking about Truvoy in the back of that security van with the steel meshing and how he'd broken Nealy's collarbone. "Thirty-six-thirty-six-thirty-six-thirty-six-thirty-six-thirty-six-thirty-six," I said to myself, counting the poles, trying to push these thoughts from my mind. I couldn't imagine how he'd done it. Did he use his *hands*, or did he *throw* Nealy against something? And why was everyone so *silent* at the table? I started to run faster and faster, clutching the book. I had to keep switching hands every fifty yards or so.

After a few hundred yards I looked behind me and I could see a car approaching. Its wipers were slashing across the windshield. I stopped in the weeds and crouched down. My breath was coming fast. After a moment the car passed and I caught my breath. I saw an old, aluminum-sided garage not far off in the distance. I headed toward it.

When I got to the garage an old codger with a tractor on his hat was leaning back in a ratty lawn chair, spitting tobacco into a brown paper bag. He sized me up and down and started laughing. His teeth looked like Indian corn. I had torn a hole in the knee of my class gray pants.

"You ain't gonna git very far, cadet," he said through the slop in his mouth. I just stood there and held on to my elbow.

"I spose you wanna use the phone," the man said. He spit into the bag. "You runners always gotta ring up a friend, right? *Come and get me Charlie. I'm freeeeeeeeee,*" he said, laughing again and pointing to a private phone that was perched on top of the hollowed-out body of an old Chevy. "It's over there. You gotta dial a niner to git out."

I walked slowly over to the phone and picked up the receiver. I didn't know who to call. I didn't even know what the hell I was doing. But I dialed nine and then zero.

"Operator," a woman said on the other end.

I didn't say anything for a second.

"Operator, can I help you?"

"Um . . ."

"Hello?"

"Can I have the area code for Philadelphia?" I asked.

She gave it to me. I hung up and picked up the phone again. I dialed nine again and then I called information for the Regency Hotel. While I waited for the number I looked over at the old man and he was humming a song with his eyes closed.

I memorized the number and called the Regency.

"Thank you for calling the Regency Hotel, how can I direct your call?"

"Um, Alice Tegroff's room, please."

After a second I could hear a quicker ring and someone picked up on the other end. It was Alice.

"Good afternoon."

"Alice?"

"Michael Jeffrey, is that *you?*"

"Hi, sis. Jesus, I'm glad you answered."

"How are you?"

"Oh. I'm . . . fine. Christ, how are you?"

"Did you get my headshot?"

"Of course," I said. "God it's good to hear your voice," I said. "How *are* you?"

"I'm *smashing*," she said in some made-up adult voice. I started to laugh like crazy.

"How are those boobs of yours?" I asked, still laughing.

"Just *wonderful*," she said in the same voice. I was laughing so hard there were tears in my eyes, but I held up pretty well.

"Wanna talk to Mom? She's right here," she asked.

"Don't tell her it's me!" I said kind of loud.

"Why?" Alice asked.

"Just don't, please?" I pleaded.

"She's in the bathroom anyway," Alice said. "She has the runs."

"How's the show going?" I asked her.

"Boring," she said. "The director's son keeps asking me out."

"Do you like him?"

"He's too horny."

"You don't even know what that *means*," I said.

"But I do."

I looked over at the old man. He was rinsing his hands with gasoline.

"How's your new *school*?" Alice asked.

"It's pretty cool," I said.

"Do you have to wear a uniform?"

"Yep."

"Do you carry a gun?"

"No, of course not."

"I'm learning how to rollerblade and I'm gonna be a vegetable librarian," she said.

"A *vegetarian?*" I said, laughing.

"Yup. I've stopped eating McDonald's and I threw a hotdog in a fountain."

"Do you miss me?" I asked.

"Of *course* I do!" she said laughing. God, it was good to hear that.

We didn't say anything to each other for a couple of seconds and then an idea came into my head.

"Hey Alice, do me a favor, willya?"

"Sure."

"Sing me that song of yours. That Little Cosette song."

"'The Castle on a *Cloud*'?"

"Yeah, that's the one. Could you sing it for me?"

"Why."

"'Cause I wanna hear it. I haven't heard it yet."

"*Okay,*" she said. "Hang on. I have to spray my throat." I could hear something spritz a few times and then she cleared her throat and started to sing. Her voice was full of vibrato.

"There is a castle on a cloud . . ."

The song was about this little girl who goes to this big castle in her dreams. And there is this lady in a white dress who holds her and sings her lullabies and tells her stories and stuff like that. For some reason, that part made me kind of sad. I cried.

When she finished, I got myself together, clapped into the phone and said a few "bravos."

"Did you put my picture in your trophy case yet?" she asked.

"Of course."

"Oh, goody," she said. "When are you coming out to see me?" she asked.

"I don't know, sis. If I came out there right now I'd get in a lotta trouble." Someone in the garage started running a motor.

"Where *are* you," Alice asked. "What's that *noise?*"

"I'm in this garage, Alice. Actually, to tell you the truth, I'm not even supposed to *be* here. I don't know what the hell I'm doing."

"Stop *swearing.*"

"Sorry."

"Well, you better not get in any trouble, Michael Jeffrey."

"I know," I said.

"And write me a letter, dumbhead."

"Okay. I will."

Then we didn't say anything for a moment. I could picture her in her hotel room with her hair up in curlers or something sophisticated like that. It made me smile.

"Listen, sis, I gotta go," I said. "I'm kinda pressed for time."

"OK. I love you."

"Me too," I said. "Don't tell Mom I called, OK?" Alice didn't respond.

"Alice, you there?"

Then the line went dead. I turned around and walked back toward the old man.

"So is Charlie on his way?" he asked.

I shook my head no.

"Need a ride to the bus station or something?"

"No thanks."

"You could call a cab," he said, looking at his greasy nails.

"I'm going back."

I went back the same way I came. I jogged about half of it and walked the rest. My elbow was still bleeding and my knee was skinned raw. The rain was coming down in an even drizzle. My book was waterlogged.

I counted telephone poles the whole way.

□ □ □

After climbing Old Shirley, I was pretty nervous. I saw some cadets leaving the mess hall but I hid behind a pile of gravel. When it was clear, I jogged around the back of the mess hall, all the way around the perimeter of the parking lot, to the other side of campus. When I reached the front gates, I casually entered. It was strange that no one saw me. I guess everyone was either still eating or walking back to the barracks.

On my way back to Glenwood Hall, I passed Spoon Benson. We both stopped at the Beacon.

"Hey, Mike," he said, saluting the Beacon. He looked a lot different in his uniform. There were three stripes on each shoulder that looked like the marks of crow feet. His shoes were shined like mirrors and his uniform was perfectly pressed. His gig line was so straight it looked as if someone had drawn it on with a ruler.

"Hi, Spoon," I said, wiping the rain out of my eyes.

"You OK?" he asked, pointing at my knee.

"Oh . . . I fell down some stairs after class."

"You might want to go to the infirmary. Looks kind of bad."

"It's nothing," I replied.

"Coach talk to you about shoes?" he asked.

"Yeah, I talked to him."

"Some of us are gonna play ball after third mess. You down with the program?"

"Sure."

"I'll try and get you on my team. Get that inside-outside game poppin' again. We'll run their asses."

"I'll be there," I said, holding my elbow. Spoon reached into his pocket and pulled out a handkerchief. He handed it to me and I wiped the blood from my arm.

"Sergeant, huh?" I asked, pointing to his stripes. Little drops of water flecked his shirt.

"Yes, sir," he said. "Squad leader." He threw his shoulders back when he said that, like he was proud of a lot of hard work. "Looks like I might get first sergeant next year if I keep my nose clean."

I handed his handkerchief back to him. For some reason, I wasn't too crazy about the way he said "first sergeant." I guess after everything that happened with Nealy and Truvoy, I had a pretty negative impression of all first sergeants.

"You sure you're OK?" he asked, wiping the rain off his stripes.

"Yeah. I'm okay. I'm fine," I said, turning to walk away.

"Hey, Mike," he said, "don't you salute the Beacon?" I didn't say anything and headed toward the entrance of Glenwood Hall.

"You should get in the habit, you know," he shouted.

I acted like I didn't hear him and just kept walking. The rain kept coming down. I couldn't seem to keep it out of my eyes.

Back in the room, I sat down at my desk. Truvoy's bed looked like the inside of an empty coffin. His closet was wide open and black with emptiness. I could see his shoes glinting a dime of light on the floor. I noticed that the scent of cocoa butter was missing. The room smelled like a dentist's office. Everything seemed so sterile.

There was a pair of shoes sitting on top of my desk. They were shined like glass all the way around. I didn't even realize they were mine until I put them on.

chapter twenty-two

Marching with a Ghost

I could barely stand the thought of sitting in my room all by myself, so after dinner I changed into my shorts, slipped on my Air Jordans, grabbed my ball, and headed over to the gym a little early.

The lights had just been turned on and the field house was pretty dim. It looked haunted, with all of the shadowy doors half open. In one spot, the floor was starting to peel and, for some reason, in the dim light, that bothered me. It's pretty sad when you look at all of those fancy brochures your dad shows you that highlight guys slam dunking basketballs and holding glossy swords, and then you run into a gym floor that has leprosy.

So I stood there for a second, staring at the chafed floor, and I started to bounce my ball. I did a figure-eight fingertip dribble between my legs a few times, and then I drove it down hard to get my hands loose. The noise echoed in the gym like a saucer shattering on a linoleum floor. Every time I'd bounce the ball, everything would shatter all over the place. I couldn't really stand the sound of that so I just stopped and sat down, holding my ball in center court. I really didn't feel like shooting or dribbling or doing defensive slides or any of that. I just wanted to sit there on the leper floor and listen to the lights buzz. I didn't even like the way my ball felt. It was all pimply and leathery. It felt like an acne-infested horse's ass, actually. I threw it out of my hands and watched it bounce toward the shadows of the entrance.

Moments later I heard doors slam and then, out of the shadows, Hufford appeared, dribbling my ball. He bounced it slowly to center court and did a really dramatic ball-handling act around me, like a vulture homing in on his prey. I didn't really pay attention to him. I really wasn't in the mood.

"One-on-one, pussy?" he asked, dribbling the ball behind his back kind of hard, so his muscles rippled. One thing I can't stand is a guy who has muscles plastered all over his body. Those stocky bastards always act like they've just pounded a gallon of Coke and come from watching that fake wrestling on TV. They're always acting so completely pumped up and macho. I guess it wouldn't be so bad if I was a little stockier. At least I'm tall, but the only halfway decent muscles on my body are on my shoulder blades, and no one ever sees your shoulder blades, except those soapy old boys in the shower who are too busy making fun of your equipment.

Anyway, Hufford was doing his vulture routine and I just ignored him, but he kept dribbling, and he started bouncing the ball close to me.

"Nice wristbands," he said. "Your mommy get you those, too?" He kept circling me and slamming my ball down close. "After I beat you I'm gonna take them from you. How 'bout that? Would you like that, Tegroff?"

I stayed silent and tried to ignore him as best I could.

"Come on, *point guard*. Lemme bust your lanky ass on the court, too. I like whippin' pussies."

I kept ignoring him, but he started slamming the ball down, really hard, about two inches away from where my hand was. In between one of the slams, he slapped me in the back of the head, and then he did it more, about four times in a row. It started to sting, and I could feel my face filling up with blood and my throat getting thick.

Then, I don't know what it was, but I stood up to him, chest to chest. I think it was the way the ball kept crashing to the floor like broken glass. He started laughing.

"Oooh. Pussy's got a red streak a mile long," he said sing-song. "Point guards are supposed to be *cool* under fire. *Temper, temper.*"

After he said that, I don't know why, but I felt my hand ball up really hard and start to cock back. Hufford was laughing right there in front of me, cracking himself up. My arm rose, and then my fist cocked back and the next thing I knew, my fist became part of Hufford's face. I punched him right in the nose, and he fell to the floor, and it had nothing to do with what he'd said about me being a point guard or having a red streak or any of that other stuff. There was blood everywhere. I think some blood even exploded on my shirt. Then after a second, I reached down and picked him up by his T-shirt with my fists. I wiped some blood that was dripping from his nose and fixed his shirt. Then I looked him directly in the eyes and filled my stomach with air.

"You know what I am, Hufford?" I asked him. I gave him a second to respond, but he was still dazed.

"I'M THE CREAM OF THE CROP," I shouted.

He just stood there staring at me. His upper lip was stuck to his braces.

I picked up my ball and walked out of the gym.

On my way back to the barracks, I spotted a kid marching alone on the guard path. It was the same kid I'd seen twice before, and he was going through the same sad routine with the rifle. In the distance, he looked really dim, like he might disappear when the sun set.

This time, I walked over to where he was marching and watched him up close for a few minutes. He looked pretty young, like he might have been a freshman. I noticed his eyes. They were probably the greenest set of eyes I'd ever seen. They didn't blink. He must've done something pretty terrible to make himself not want to blink, I thought.

Then, I don't know why, I guess it was because of the great mood I was in, I decided to march with him. I just waited for him to stop and complete one of those jackknife moves with the rifle, and I flanked his left. When he started to march, so did I, right next to him, in my gym clothes, with my ball slung under my arm. He didn't say anything to me and I didn't say anything to him. We just marched together in silence, under the balmy sky, and I felt pretty good. I think he did too, because out of the corner of my eye I could see that he was blinking. His green eyes were fluttering like crazy and even though he didn't know me from a can of paint, I don't think he was as scared anymore. And maybe I wasn't either.

chapter twenty-three

Poking Through

I stood in the dark, shadowy part of my room by the closets, where the light doesn't quite make it from the window. I looked in Truvoy's closet and saw his shoes. I picked them up. They felt nice in my hands. There were a lot of cracks his feet had formed. Although my shoes were pretty new, there were the same kinds of cracks already etching themselves into the leather. I looked at my shoes. My cracks didn't run quite as deep as Truvoy's and they branched in different directions. I guess nobody could have exactly the same kinds of cracks as yours. It made me feel good to know that my shoes were still forming their patterns and that they wouldn't be like anyone else's.

Then I took off my Air Jordans and tried on Truvoy's low quarters. Although they were a couple of sizes too big, they really didn't feel too bad. I walked around the room. I started to walk really fast and goofy, in little circles and figure eights. I probably looked really demented. For a second, I walked like a chicken, then I did a little German Smurfing, and I even stopped by the sink, vibrated my can, and tried to get a little booty.

After putting Truvoy's shoes back in his closet, I looked over at my desk and saw the piece of stationery with the fish on it, and I realized that I'd never written that letter to Alice. I walked over to my desk, opened the top drawer and saw those two other letters I'd written: the one to Charlie and the one to Mom and Alice. I put some stamps on them and placed them on top of my desk. Then I took out a blank envelope and wrote Dad's address on the front and thought about writing him a letter, too.

There was a knock on my door. I looked up and Hillcrest was standing in the entrance with a piece of paper in his hand. I stood at attention.

"You're wanted in the Commandant's office," he said. He walked into the room, placed the note on my bed and started to walk out. He stopped at the entrance of my closet and looked down at my low quarters.

"Not bad," he said.

◻ ◻ ◻

On my way to the Commandant's office, I dropped the letters in the outgoing mail slot. I was nervous as hell. I had hoped to God that nobody had seen me on that road while I was AWOL. Or maybe Hillcrest had written me up for running out of the mess hall. I couldn't keep my hands from shaking.

I knocked on the door and then I heard a woman's voice tell me to take a seat on the wooden benches, that someone would be with me shortly. Those benches were really uncomfortable. All over the surface, kids had carved their initials with their graduating class next to them. L.B. '78, K. North '81, Smiley '66 were just some of them. I couldn't imagine the number of cadets who had sat on this bench and gotten the third degree from the Commandant. And who was this guy anyway? I pictured him with scars on his face and an eye patch. Or maybe he had a wooden leg and a hook for a hand?

I thought about adding my initials to the bench, but I didn't have anything sharp on me.

"Tegroff, front and center!" a gravelly voice blurted from inside the office. My stomach just about dropped to the floor. I stood at attention in

front of the entrance. A bald-headed man was turned around in a huge leather chair, facing the window.

"Sir, cadet recruit Tegroff requests permission to enter the office, sir!"

"At ease," the man said. I stood at parade rest with my hands fixed to the small of my back. My knees were shaking pretty bad. He turned around in his chair. His nametag said Col. Beane, and he looked kind of like Don Zimmer, former manager of the Chicago Cubs. He smoked a filterless cigarette, I think Lucky Strikes. There were yellow nicotine stains all over his fingers.

"So I hear you're quite a basketball prospect," he said, exhaling a plume of smoke, then placing the cigarette in an ashtray.

"Yes, sir," is all I could think of to say.

"You know, Tegroff, I was the head of Military Science at Indiana when Isiah Thomas was there," Colonel Beane said as he grabbed his Zippo lighter and started flipping the top.

I just looked front.

"That kid was quick as a damn gnat," he said.

"Yes, sir."

"One time I saw him shake this kid from Notre Dame so bad he broke his ankle."

"Sir, wow, sir," I said. He kept at it with the lighter for a minute and then he finally stopped and put it down.

"He sure had some moves," Colonel Beane said, retrieving his cigarette, dragging heavily so the ember blazed red for a long time, and then exhaling, filling the entire office with a fog of smoke. I coughed a few times. I'm not very good with cigarette smoke. Colonel Beane crushed it out in the ashtray.

"So, Tegroff, you like it here at St. Matthew's so far?" he asked, already pulling a new Lucky Strike out of the pack. He tapped one of the ends on the back of his wrist a few times and then slipped it between his narrow lips.

"Yes, sir," I said. I was really trying to say the right things.

"You sure about that?"

"Absolutely, sir. I'm *sure*, sir."

"You like the chow?"

"Um, yes, sir."

"Good," he said with the cigarette still dangling from his mouth, unlit. "That's good, because the chow's good here. It'll make you strong as a damn Clydesdale." Then he stood up and looked out his window.

"We turn out some good men. You know that, don't you, Tegroff?"

"Yes, sir."

"And you look like you could be one of them. If you keep your nose clean. What do you think?"

"Oh, absolutely, sir."

"Do you mind if I smoke this one?" he asked, turning around and sitting back down.

"Oh, absolutely not, sir."

"Thanks," he said lighting up again. "I tried that goddamn patch thing but all that did was make me crave Band-Aids," Colonel Beane said, inhaling, his cheeks caving in with suction.

"You know why I called you down here, Tegroff?" he asked, blowing it through his nose.

"No, sir."

"You've probably been wondering, right?"

"Yes, sir."

"Well, I just wanted to let you know that your father isn't gonna be able to make it next weekend. He wanted me to tell you that he's sorry, and that he couldn't change his plans."

"Yes, sir."

"He asked when our first basketball game was, though. I told him it was our Thanksgiving Tip-off. We usually play Geldon in the first round. The

Geldon Caxy's. You know what a Caxy is, Tegroff?"

"No, sir."

"It's a mythological frog. Whattaya think of that for school mascot?" he asked.

"I think it sounds pretty half-baked, sir."

"Nice way of puttin' it," he said. Then he laughed a few times to himself. My knees finally stopped shaking.

"Is that okay with you, Tegroff?" Colonel Beane asked. "That I told your father that?"

"Yes, sir!" I said.

"Good, 'cause he's coming."

"Thank you, sir," I said.

"Those are damn good shoes, cadet," he said, leaning over his desk and pointing to my low quarters.

"Thank you, sir."

"I think I'll give you a merit. How would you like that, Tegroff?"

"Yes, sir!" I said. He put his cigarette in the ashtray, wrote something on a piece of paper and folded it in half.

"Who's your squad leader?" he asked.

"Sergeant Hillcrest, sir." He wrote Hillcrest's name on the front.

"Well, when you get back to the barracks, you

give this to Hillcrest. Maybe he'll give you some TV privileges or something."

"Thank you, sir," I said.

"Dismissed."

"Sir, cadet recruit Tegroff requests permi—"

"Get outta here," he said before I could finish. He had a smile on his face.

I had some time to kill before study hours, so after I gave the piece of paper to Hillcrest (he said I could study in the TV lounge if I wanted), I decided to go over and say hi to Mr. Savery. I knocked on his door a couple of times. I heard some muffled music playing and then it stopped. He opened the door. There was a guitar in his hand.

"Hey. There he is," he said with a guitar pick in between his teeth. He was wearing a paint-splattered sweatshirt and a pair of jeans.

"Thought I'd just stop by to say hi," I said.

"Well, come on in."

His apartment was full of books and boxes and clothes, and there were plants everywhere.

"Sorry about the mess. It takes me a while to get settled. The place I just moved from never seemed to evolve out of the box stage," he said, showing me to his living room. "Want something to drink?

I have water, milk, and water," he said jokingly. "You can have the water hot or cold."

"No, thanks. I'm fine."

On a shelf by his TV there were a bunch of gold basketball trophies. "What are all these for?" I asked.

"Free throws," he said. "I was the Pepsi Hot Shot National Freethrow Champion in 1979. I had a court in my backyard. It was like my little cathedral. Whenever I had something bothering me, I'd just go out back and spend hours at the charity stripe."

"I do that, too," I said.

"I'd even shovel the court off in the winter, and my ball would get all flat from the cold air."

"You gotta soak it in hot water when that happens," I said.

"I know," he said. "My buddies and I used to use two balls and my mom would boil water for us and we'd alternate."

"I used to shoot with snowmobile gloves," I said.

"Oh, you have to try *batting* gloves," Mr. Savery said. "Much more control with those."

"Wow," I said.

"When it got dark out, I'd just turn the floodlights on from my dad's old Jeep," Mr. Savery said.

"Did you play college ball anywhere?" I asked.

"Nope. Everyone thought I was two steps too slow. I could shoot the lights out, but I wasn't quick enough to defend guards on the college level. And I couldn't jump out of my own shoes. I sure as hell could hit those free throws, though."

Then he drummed on the front of his guitar with his thumbs and smiled.

"So . . . your parents coming up for the big weekend?" he asked.

"Um, no."

"Well, you're welcome to hang out here if you can stand the mess. What kind of music do you like?"

"I guess I like pretty much everything. Rap especially."

"How 'bout Simon and Garfunkel? They're not exactly hip-hop, but they'd definitely make my all-star team."

"Yeah, sure. I can handle that," I said.

He sat down on the floor Indian style and started playing his guitar. He was really good. I sat down on his couch that was full of newspapers and a couple of towels and just tried to get comfortable. He sang this song called "The Boxer" about a poor boy who leaves his family and goes out to New York City.

Mr. Savery had a pretty nice voice, and the way the guitar kind of mixed in with his singing made me feel really good. I just lounged back in between all of his newspapers and clothes, with my head resting on the back of his couch, and let the music wash over me. I closed my eyes and just let my head go clear.

I pictured my mountaintop, with the swirling clouds, and the piano, and my goat. I was just lying in the grass, petting my goat, who was snacking on a tin can. He *baa*ed a couple of really nice *baas* and smiled that special way a goat can smile, and then, from under his beard, he offered me a bottle of lotion. I squirted some into the palm of my hand. It smelled all nice and cocoa buttery. Then I pulled up my pant legs and started massaging it into my calves. Then my goat turned to me and said "Why the heck do you use so much lotion?" and I told him something about the salt in my sweat making my skin dry out. I told him it was so I wouldn't get *ashy*. I worked the lotion into both legs, and the whole mountaintop started to smell all sweet and cocoa buttery, just like an old friend.

Then I stood up and walked over to my piano and lifted the lid and looked at the keys, which were all clean and polished. The clouds were really thick and gray, and they were hanging low. Then, for some reason, I stood on the bench and walked onto the top of the piano. The breeze felt nice on my face, and everything was really foggy and swirly. I stood up as tall as I could, stretched my neck as high as possible, and poked my head right through the clouds.

Then I looked around at the rest of the world and I saw the most amazing thing: for what seemed like hundreds of miles, there were zillions of other mountaintops, with clouds swirling and goats *baa*ing, and kids hanging out. Some of them were petting their goats, some of them were just lying in the grass, and some of them were standing on top of their pianos, poking their heads through the clouds, looking around at the rest of the world, just like me. It was the most amazing thing I'd ever seen.

After a while, I sat down on the piano bench, looked over at my goat, and started to press down on the keys, first slowly, and then faster and faster, and all of this music started coming out of my hands like I'd been practicing for years and I'd just forgotten how to play. It was like magic; the most wonderful magic. It wasn't anything dramatic like Beethoven's Fifth or the "Castle on a Cloud," but it sounded really nice.

"Mike . . . Mike. Earth to Mike. You still with me?" Mr. Savery said, with his hand on my shoulder.

"Yeah," I said. "I'm still here."

"I thought you were in a trance for a second there. You looked pretty peaceful."

"You know, Mr. Savery . . ." I said, still hearing some of that music in the back of my mind.

"Yeah?"

I started to think about all the things I wanted to talk about, about how I was going to tough it out and all of that, but I knew I would have plenty of time. *Just take it slow.*

"I can run one helluva fast break."

He looked at me, pulled his guitar close, and started to play another song.

I could feel myself slowly nodding my head. Yes.

ADAM RAPP was born in Chicago, Illinois. An alumnus of St. John's Military Academy in Delafield, Wisconsin, he has a B.A. in Writing from Clarke College, where he was captain of the basketball team. He lives in New York City with his dog, Scooter. *Missing the Piano* is his first novel.